Unlik

Friends

VICKY KASEORG

ISBN-13: 978-1535374101
ISBN-10: 1535374101

Cover Painting: Vicky Kaseorg
Cover Design: Perry Elisabeth Design
Editor: Amy Fox

Chapter One

Some people think I'm smart, but I quickly disabuse them of that notion. I would never use the word disabuse in front of them either. I don't need nobody thinking I'm smart and having expectations. Expectations nearly always lead to disappointment.

So when I tell folks the story about my three best friends, Flash, Zippy, and Lightning, they all think I am making it up or, more likely, just plain stupid. They laugh right in my face and tell me only a dimwit would think a dolphin, a dog, and a horse could be best friends. Maybe the dog and horse. There are plenty of videos of that. But a dolphin thrown in the mix? No way.

So I want you to know right off the bat, as long as you don't spread it around, I am not dumb. I only mention that so you will trust that this story is not a half-baked casserole of ideas from an addled brain. Sometimes I wonder why I bother since no one believes me and everyone ridicules me.

But it's a story that has to be told. Miracles like this one just don't show up every day. The message is one that can change a life. Leastways, it changed mine. I figured it could change someone else's too.

First, some introduction so you know who you are dealing with. My name is Leah Grace. I am eighteen years old and lived on my own for two years in an abandoned single-wide trailer. The windows were busted out, and the door was a flap of old carpet I stapled to the door jamb when I first moved in. It was all the shelter I needed living in Florida along one of the snaky, murky waterways. It almost never leaks below freezing here.

More about the palace I lived in later. We can bog down in those boring details when things get too exciting.

I am the only daughter of a drunk and a drug addict. I know. Bet you're jealous. I ran away when I was sixteen. Ran is not actually the right word. Strolled away would describe my locomotion better. The blessed parents were both in a typical collapsed heap of snoring, jelly-like blobs of smelly flesh. They never knew I left. They never came looking for me either. Or if they did, they didn't look very far or very hard. They certainly never found me. For which I thank God. Who may or may not be real. This story definitely tipped the scale to the maybe side, rather than maybe not.

Since I was sixteen, and of legal age to drop out of school, no one from the Education Department came hunting me down. Not that I expected them too. I had burned all the bridges and then some with regards to making many friends in that establishment.

Like I said, it isn't that I am dumb, though I would consider myself only marginally educated. I was even briefly considered for the gifted and talented program (G and T) till I ended up in the Juvenile Delinquent jail. Which wasn't my fault. That was a classic case of wrong place, wrong time, but no one believed me. You don't want to hear that story right now. Trust me.

Suffice it to say I am smart, but not to the casual observer and not to the Department of Education either. They said if I was smart I wouldn't have ended up in jail. Due to being underage, I got sent to a special school that specialized in fixing bad kids, instead of making me break boulders at Alcatraz with a ball and chain around my ankle.

I would stay till the moment I could legally escape. I did the minimal required work, which led them to reconsider the G and T label, and put me in Remedial Classes instead. One teacher went to bat for me, catching a whiff of my subterfuge. She heard me use a word just like subterfuge and pulled me aside. She told me to 'fess up' because she knew I was not living up to my potential. No one comes up with subterfuge by accident. I told her I was exceeding my potential, and was just lucky to have mastered my ABC's.

That was not true. I could read like a doctoral student. I spent every spare minute I had reading, while not dodging my father's fists or my mother's frying pan aimed at my head. I taught myself to read while I was still in diapers. I bet you think that's a fib too like this whole story about the dolphin, dog, and horse…but it is the truth. Who else was gonna teach me? Unless it was reading the fine print, Pregnant women should not consume alcohol, which was printed on all my mother's reading material. (Which by the way, she clearly didn't read…or leastways didn't heed.) If I wanted to learn to read, I had to take matters into my own hands.

I hated school, but I loved its library. The librarian, Miss Gribbs, was the one other adult on God's green earth who thought I had potential, but she couldn't convince any of the others. Especially because while I knew how to act like I wasn't a blubbering idiot, I never did because then I'd have to live up to what others figured I should be capable of. It was an art, talking like a moron. It's harder than you think, unless you are one. Then it's a piece of cake. I actually had to work at it. You'll probably notice I switch in and out of sounding like a hillbilly. When I forget myself, I can sound like a Harvard graduate. Subterfuge is not nearly the fanciest word I know.

I felt bad that I didn't let on to Miss Gribbs what I was really all about. She was nice, and really wanted to help me. I shoulda at least told her goodbye, but I didn't. I turned sixteen, packed all my worldly goods, which fit in my purse, and headed south. It took every ounce of mercy that I didn't kick my parents' inert bodies as I stepped over them on my way out the door.

Fortunately for me, I was born with some useful features. Thick straight blonde hair, the color of sunshine. Green eyes that could turn blue if it was a cloudless day. Fast metabolism that kept me thin, even if the constant lack of food had not. I was not proud of my nice features, since I had nothing to do with them. They were issued to me by God or random evolutionary chance at birth. They landed me in a whole lot more trouble than I would have liked, but they sure were useful at times.

I committed a sin early on, because I had to. I stole a nice shirt and pants so I could get a job. My good looks, which I only mention so you understand the story, in conjunction with that stolen interview outfit snagged me a position at the local Better-Mart. Right away, I got me a P.O. box so I had a legal address for Better-Mart to send my checks. I had taken a wad of my dear parents' hard earned money from drug peddling which paid for the P.O. box, and my travel expenses.

I didn't think Better-Mart would consent to sending my pay to "the abandoned rusted single-wide on the second big bend of the Suwannee after the little town of Kumsquat." (I think Kumsquat is a Native American word for Cesspool. Leastways, that's what it looked like.)

By the way, don't count taking that money as a sin. It was my inheritance. Since I didn't plan on seeing my folks again in this lifetime, I'd prefer you call it foresight and shrewd financial planning. Sounds better than robbery.

Now before you start thinking this story has all the makings of a tall-tale, I did have access to a place to clean up and get fresh water. My plush abode was all by itself in an abandoned field that was right next to the curvy Suwannee River. Since it tended to flood, no one ever ventured there. But I just had to walk a quarter mile through some snake infested reeds across the vacant lot, cross a lazy street, and there was a run-down campground and RV park. The Kumsquat Oasis, they called it. What a load of crock that name was!

While oasis was a bit of a stretch, it did have a decent bathhouse. If I timed it right, I could use the central bath house and no one was ever the wiser.

I may have come from the dregs of humanity, but I had some self-respect. I stayed clean, and I kept a nice house. It was always picked up and neat in my single-wide. That wasn't hard because I had all of three possessions to work around. #1: A couch that came with my sweet little home, which spewed out musty vapors if I plopped down too hard on it. That doubled as my bed. #2: A Coleman stove which I bought with my first Better-Mart paycheck. #3: One pan. I cooked and ate out of the same pan. Saved on dishes.

I kept a jug of water which I filled at the Kumsquat Oasis RV park. I always washed the pan immediately so it was ready for the next meal. Since I had no refrigerator, or electricity…I never could store any food but that wasn't a problem. I worked full-time, after the first few weeks of getting my bearings, and on the way home from Better-Mart, stopped and picked up whatever I needed for the next day. Until then, I basically starved. Starving is not so hard when you are used to it. Which I was.

At first, this was not an easy life. I won't go into details about those early days because it would make you cry and this story is not a mournful one. There was a lot of walking and biking involved, until I had enough money from my Better-Mart job to use the bus. This is an important thing to point out not to make you feel sorry for me but to set the stage for the first miracle.

I was sulking in my little patch of swamp when I heard something snuffling outside my door.

This was during my pre-employment stage, and things looked mighty grim. I peeked around the old flap of carpet, hoping it wasn't a carnivore of some sort. You will not believe what to my wondering eyes should appear.

A horse. She was a skinny nag, though just shy of starving. She had a faded blue halter on her head. Judging from her condition, she had been on her own a while. Instant affinity towards her! She was in the same dire straits as me.

She munched on the tall reeds around my patch of heaven. I didn't know horses could eat swamp reeds but she was evidently enjoying her breakfast. She was a bright yellowish white. Leastways she would've been if she didn't have a half acre of reddish mud all over her. I called her Lightning right away. Not 'cause of any flash of speed or electric spirit. Just on account of her color. It was a little bit of a semantic joke. Like Kumsquat Oasis. She was as about un-Lightning as a horse could be. Poor thing.

When I poked my head around the flap of carpet, she looked up. Her jaw was munching in a circular pattern, just as contentedly as if she were in a rich green grass pasture. She gazed at me without the slightest bit of fear. We had an instant connection.

"Hello. I'm Leah."

Lightning looked straight at me without blinking, interested in what I had to say. I hadn't spoken to a soul for a few weeks. I'd been hiding out in my single-wide, and stealing food from the trailer park convenience store. When they began noticing me, I snatched sustenance from the Family Dollar instead.

Oh yeah. I forgot to mention that earlier. There were two sins before I snagged the Better-Mart job. I think that is all, but I could be forgetting some. They were not easy days at first, and starvation has a way of playing with your memory.

The horse watched me a little longer, and then decided I was safe. She lowered her head and began ripping at the reedy grass again. I crept down the rusty aluminum stairs by my door, which as you recall was not a door but a carpet flap, and slowly walked towards her. Or him. I don't know much about horses and couldn't really tell at first. Ok, her. As I got closer I confirmed my first impression was correct.

She didn't panic at all as I approached. She was the first horse I had ever come to within fifty feet of. You would think I'd be afraid, but I was getting lonesome by then, having run away only a couple of weeks prior, and being all on my own. Not that my parents were much company, or even much protection. Still. They were at least contact with another being of sorts.

I think Lightning felt the same way I did. What I know about horses could be stuffed in a jelly bean, but why else was a wild horse munching tough reeds in my swamp when she could go anywhere?

I moved very slowly, since I had no idea what to expect with a horse. I probably should have been afraid, but I wasn't. Lightning looked to be a peaceable sort.

Soon, I was standing right in front of her. At that point she lifted her head, and paused in her chewing. Her ears snapped forward, and she gave me a good once over. Then she stuck her nose right in my belly and blew out a long stream of warm moist air from her nostrils. It tickled.

I reached out, a little tentative at first, and touched her nose. Later I would learn that was called a muzzle but I didn't know it then. It was about the softest thing I had ever felt.

Lightning closed her eyes, and recommenced chewing. She looked content as I petted her soft muzzle. As I stroked her neck, breaking away clods of the caked red mud, I immediately began plotting how to keep her with me. I didn't have anything like a rope. The only material I had were the clothes I was wearing, and I sure couldn't sacrifice them.

I glanced at the fibrous reeds Lightning was digesting. I could maybe braid those into a rope, but it would take a while, and even then, I doubted it would be strong enough to hold a horse.

Honestly, I don't know what I was thinking. I wasn't hardly in a position to own a pet, let alone a horse. I was only barely surviving on my own. Still, I had never had anything of value, and never a friend in the world. This horse had looked on me with more kindness than anyone except maybe Miss Gribbs, the librarian.

It dawned on me then that the last thing I should do was keep Lightning by force. If she wanted to stay with me, I would find a way to take care of her. But I wouldn't tie her up so she had no choice. That didn't seem like the way a real friend would behave…even if I had a rope. Which I didn't.

I sat down on the ground in front of Lightning, since I didn't have any pressing duties to rush off to. While she munched the reeds, we communed. Every so often, she would pause in her grazing, and nibble at my knee. It was very companionable. I was the happiest I'd ever been in my life.

Chapter Two

Now that I had a horse to provide for, I decided I needed income. If it weren't for the appearance of Lightning, I might have just sat in that single-wide staring at the ebb and flow of the Suwannee till I starved to death. They'd have found my bones sitting on the aluminum stoop of the trailer.

'Cause that is what I did every moment I could spare. Which at first, was all of them. I sat on the stoop looking out at the winding waterway. I began to learn about high tide and low tide. Not that it would take a genius. Which I wasn't.

At high tide, the water came to within fifty feet of my abode. It covered half-way up the reeds. At low tide, it was maybe twenty feet further away, maybe more at times. The water got real shallow then. Little critters, which I later discovered were shrimp, jumped right out of the water, especially at low tide.

Sometimes, very, very rarely, a fisherman glided by in a row boat or small motor boat. I always hid out behind my flap of carpet till he passed by. No sense attracting notice. Mostly, I saw no one.

The first morning after I met Lightning, I leaped out of bed with the first wisp of hope I'd felt in a decade or so. Maybe ever. Would Lightning still be there???

I flew around the carpet flap and down the stairs. *No horse.* My heart sank deeper than China, which I hear is all the way down and out the other side of the planet.

I moped for a second, and then slowly traipsed around the corner of the trailer. You could not believe how relieved I was to see Lightning just around the corner, soaking up the morning sun. That's when I knew I had a forever friend.

At that moment, I formulated a plan. This would be my home, but it could use a few modernizing touches. If I were going to stay here, I needed income. I had to find a job.

Looking down at my tattered duds sparked an epiphany. (Nice word, huh?) I needed an interview outfit and this wasn't it. There was a Family Dollar just outside the trailer park. It took a bit of stealth, but I managed to snag a decent polo shirt and black stretchy pants without alerting the authorities. One thing I did learn from my parents was how to make a living without spending a cent.

No one would blame me if I decided to follow in their footsteps and put all their fine tutoring in the art of living off the street to good use. To tell you the truth, I don't know myself why I didn't. All I knew was that I wanted to earn my keep. I wasn't stealing from anyone by staying in the trailer. No one else seemed to want it. But I didn't want to steal to feed or clothe myself. I wanted self-respect, which I had never really owned, but decided it was worth having.

So, I delayed my self-respect long enough to pilfer the interview outfit. I hoped my grimy sandals would pass for interview shoes. The next day, I went back to the Family Dollar and stuffed a bar of soap and a hairbrush under my shirt.

I took only what was absolutely necessary. Unless you count the Milky Way. I probably should have left that behind. During high tide, I took my bar of soap and washed up in the Suwannee. I didn't know about the Kumsquat Oasis bathhouse yet.

I scrubbed myself, and my clothes. I hung my clothes to dry on the stoop, and decided I'd get to braiding reeds that very day for a clothes line. Braided reed might not hold a horse, but I bet it would hold a skinny girl's shorts and t-shirt.

While my clothes were drying in the hot sun, I hid out in the trailer. No sense sitting buck naked on the stoop, courting trouble. I did peek out every so often and whistle to Lightning. I wanted her to know I was still there.

She plodded right over when I whistled. I poked my head around the carpet square door when I heard her hooves clomping on the ground. She blinked at me, and I could tell she was wondering why I'd called.

"I just needed to know you were still here," I told her.

She twitched her ears to let me know she had heard me, and understood. I darted a look around to see if any boats were on the horizon. Since there weren't any, I scurried down the steps and checked my duds. Bone dry.

Florida sunshine could fry an egg in a minute, and so lots of folks don't like it, but it was better than an electric dryer. Considering my plight, that was a good thing.

I put on my freshly washed duds, and felt like a new person. Mud and grime really deflate one's self-image.

"You wait here," I told Lightning. "I need to do some exploring. If we are going to stay here, I'm gonna need some supplies. And for supplies, I need a job."

Lightning tossed her head like she got my drift. I figured the first thing I needed to do was set out and find a business close enough to walk to that was likely to hire me. Walking was the only free mode of transportation I had. I was a little worried about going back to the Family Dollar in my newly pilfered interview outfit. I hoped I'd find another place that would hire me not too much further down the road.

I carefully folded my interview outfit and laid it as flat as possible in my purse. I could be walking a long way, and I didn't want it to get all smelly and dirty. I would find a place to change if I found a good place to interview.

I bet you think I had a snowball's chance in hell of having all I would need for a job. Like a Social Security card. Remember I warned you that if I wanted, I could be smart? This proves it. Before I skedaddled from my folks, along with my inheritance I picked up the single envelope of my valuable papers. It had my SS card, my birth certificate, and my baby footprints. I think when I was born my mama had a moment of excitement, and gathered all those precious things in an old used envelope. It was lucky for me she did because I snagged them on my way out the door with foresight that even amazed me, and I *do* know my true potential.

As soon as I started walking, Lightning set in right behind me, matching me step for step. I stopped. She stopped.

"Now you can't come along," I told her. "Where would I park you if I go in for an interview?"

Lightning didn't answer, but she didn't back away either. And as soon as I headed back towards the road, she clip-clopped right on my heels.

"Well, maybe this will just be a reconnaissance mission," I said after several futile attempts to turn her back. I stretched my arm across her neck, and we walked companionably across the reedy field.

Like I said, it was hot. Pretty soon, I was mighty thirsty, dripping sweat, and tired. Lightning musta been used to the climate, because she didn't seem to mind it at all. That gave me an idea.

I didn't know much about horses, but I knew people rode them. I had never been on a horse, and knew nothing about riding, but I figured since Lightning had a halter, someone musta tamed her at some point.

Ignorance is bliss. Perhaps you have heard that. I know climbing on the back of a horse you just met might be considered ignorance by some. And ok, it was. But I lucked out. Lightning didn't mind at all. She stood completely still while I tried to wiggle my way up on top of her.

She was not very tall, but anyone who tells you climbing on to a horse is easy is lying. Don't buy any bridges from them. I did manage, but not without a heap of trouble.

Next problem. I was sitting proud as could be on top of her, but I didn't have the sprinkling of an idea of how to make her go.

"Giddyup," I said. I had seen that in cartoons. It's what they always said to horses when they wanted them to move out. Lightning must not have watched those cartoons because it didn't have the slightest effect on her.

I leaned over and snapped off a tall reed. Then I swished it over her ears. She tossed her head, and turned to glare at me. Still no forward progress. I smacked it on her rump, which would hurt about as much as a feather. That did the trick! She started walking in the general direction of the road.

A little trial and error of reaching forward and tugging on her halter worked to guide her to some degree. It wasn't easy. I had to climb part way up her neck to do it, but she didn't seem to mind. I figured I could braid some reeds to make reins when we got home. *If* we got home.

See, at that moment, she decided to trot. I don't know what set her off. Maybe nothing. Maybe she just thought it was time for some exercise. Whatever her reason, she didn't warn or consult me. So I crashed against her neck, and then bounced way back, and would've slid off except I managed to snatch some mane on my flight to her butt. I hung on, barely, and crawled my way back to her shoulders. Then I clung, double fisted, to her mane.

This turned out to be a blessing in disguise. By gripping her mane with both hands, I realized that if I tugged on one side, pulling her neck in that direction, it made her turn that way. If I pulled to the other side, same little miracle of horse steering! I seriously doubt that is how most people steer. I bet it isn't even called steering. But it worked.

Once she hit the road, she slowed to a walk. My brains were scrambled good by then. My eyeballs were probably rolling around in their sockets. I used my new directional cues to head her past the Kumsquat Oasis and on to 'town'.

Kumsquat city limits is one of those places where you better not blink or you miss it. It was hardly a roaring metropolis. This was good because I am not even sure if it was legal for me to ride a horse down the street. Some folks stopped and stared. Not many, since there was only a handful of people out and about.

We passed a hole-in-the-wall diner, a tattoo shop, a small grocery store, and a barber shop. That was it for the businesses in town. The Family Dollar was in a small shopping center across from Kumsquat Oasis. There was a Family Practice Medical center in that plaza and a drugstore. Oh, the Post Office was there too, which was good since it was pretty convenient to get to my mailbox.

It took us all of five minutes to make it to the outer limits of Kumsquat. Lightning seemed content to amble along on the dusty edge of the road, so I settled into her rhythm, and hoped we would eventually pass a place that looked like it was not on the verge of bankruptcy.

This is the eerie part. She kept walking while I daydreamed, and looked about at the desolate countryside, when we passed a billboard announcing really exciting news. A brand new Better-Mart was one mile ahead. There was a banner diagonally across the bottom right hand corner. "Grand Opening, May 15th!"

Honestly, I had no idea exactly what day it was, but I knew I had left my folks sometime in late April. I tried to count down the days since I'd been on my own, but finally gave up. I figured it was at least three weeks.

It wasn't. When I arrived, the sign on the door said, "Closed. Grand Opening, May 15." Some workmen planting bushes in planters along the sidewalk gaped at me. You would think they'd never seen a horse at Better-Mart before.

I took a major chance.

"What day is it?" I asked.

They laughed, and poked each other in the ribs, like I was some sort of circus show. One of them elbowed his friend, and said, "Shut up, Mack. It's May 13, pretty girl."

"They hiring?" I asked.

"They already got all the horses they need," Mack said, and then doubled over laughing like he was God's gift to comedy.

"Shut up Mack!" his friend said, again. "You can ask. That door over there leads to the office."

Fortunately, that door was way off to the corner away from those barrels of fun (not). I didn't even have to tell Lightning to move on. It was like she read my mind. I steered her around the corner.

First thing I had to do was change into my interview outfit. Then I had to figure out how to tie Lightning safely out of view. We plodded all the way to the back, which was deserted. I slipped off Lightning, and after triple checking, changed into my interview clothes in record time.

Then pure genius wrapped its hands around my brain. I unhooked the strap from my purse, hooked one end to the halter, and the other end to a tree branch.

"Stay," I told Lightning. She closed her eyes.

If she decided she didn't want to stay, that flimsy hook on the strap and the tiny tree branch wasn't gonna hold her. I knew that, and she knew that. But I had no choice. I had to go get a job or things looked mighty dire for me.

When I rounded the corner, the men were busy with their tree planting, and didn't notice me. I slipped quickly through the door to the office.

Following signs, I made my way to a windowless room just big enough for one desk and two chairs. A woman was working at a computer.

"May I help you?" she asked when I knocked on the open door.

"I'm here for a job."

"Did you fill out an application?" she asked.

"No. Where do I get one of them?"

"I can give you one. I am afraid all our positions are filled however. You can fill one out, and we will call you."

I looked at her, all hope crashing down. Slim pickin's of employment opportunities resided in Kumsquat. And how was she going to call me? I didn't have a phone.

I shoulda said something, and normally I am pretty quick on my feet, but I couldn't think of a thing to say. To make matters worse, a big tear plopped out of my eye, all by itself.

She musta noticed because as she handed me the application, a soft look crossed her face, like she felt sorry for me. I wasn't trying to get her pity. I couldn't help it. I'd gone three weeks without much to eat, and I'd been dreaming about starting work that very day and buying a real meal at the Kumsquat diner. Stupid, I know.

"Do you have experience?" she asked.

"Yes ma'am. Tons."

"Well that's great! Have you worked in Better-Mart before?"

"No."

"What is your experience in?"

This question stymied me. I thought at first she was asking if I had experience, as in life experiences. I had those out to wazoo. How many kids my age had learned to fend for themselves since they were old enough to walk? Not many. Oh the stories I could tell her!

But then I realized, she probably wasn't looking for *that* kind of experience.

"She can ride a horse without a saddle or reins," a deep voice said behind me.

I swung around. It was the same man that had smacked Mack and told him to shut up.

"Oh?" the lady said, "Did you ride a horse here?"

"Yeah. She's parked out back. I hope that's okay."

The man and the woman exchanged glances.

"I assume you are looking for part time work, after school?" asked the lady.

"Oh no. I finished school." I didn't tell her that they finished with me, though that was more accurate. "I want full time work. And I will work hard."

"Nancy," the man said, "There is something I need to talk with you about real quick. Privately."

Nancy nodded. She handed me a pen and the application. "I will be right back. Go ahead and fill this out."

She stepped out with the man, and they whispered just outside the door. I didn't exactly eavesdrop, but I have better than average hearing. It's a skill I developed trying to keep my parents from beating the crap out of me when they came stumbling in drunk or high. I could hear them coming from three blocks away and discern from the sounds of their footsteps if they were sober, or if I needed to go into hiding.

"She changed her clothes behind the building….homeless….wretched skinny horse…."

Oh-oh. I think my cover was blown. I kept filling out the forms, but was planning my escape. Last thing I needed was them grabbing me and handing me over to social services.

When Nancy stepped back in, she looked over my application.

"You're just sixteen?" she asked.

I nodded.

She pointed to my address. The post office box.

"My parents just moved," I lied, "So they use the post office box so no mail gets lost in the shuffle."

I thought this was brilliant, especially on the fly. I am not sure if Nancy bought it but she moved on, reading the rest of the application.

"Honey," she said, with a sigh, "Are you on your own?"

I weighed my thoughts carefully. If I admitted that, I was a goner. She knew something was fishy. I decided to tell the truth. A partial truth.

"I'm staying in an RV with friends. You know the Kumsquat Oasis?"

She nodded.

"I really need this job. My parents are drug addicts and my friends are great, but I have to make my own way. I can't stay with them forever."

Nancy could have reported me to DSS. She probably should have. I don't know why she decided to pretend she believed me. She nodded again, and then she said, "We open Tuesday. I think we can make a place for you as a cashier. Can you be here at 8 a.m. Monday for the training session?"

I think my mouth was hanging open. I never expected to get the job.

"I would not recommend riding the horse here each day," she told me. "There is a bus stop right outside the Kumsquat Oasis."

"Yes ma'am. Thank you!"

There were more forms to sign, and she gave me a packet of Better-Mart policies. I didn't even ask how much I would be making. It didn't matter. It had to be a whole lot more than nothing.

When I raced out the door, and back around the corner, my heart was bursting with joy. I was also worried. Would Lightning still be there?

She was! She was standing right where I left her, eyes still closed, enjoying the shade of the building blocking the brutal sun. Again, I checked for any peeping Toms, and when I'd assured myself it was safe, I switched back into my riding outfit. Carefully folding my interview suit, I put it back in my purse. Then I unsnapped the strap from the tree, but kept it attached to the halter. One rein was better than none!

Chapter Three

Lightning made it home with barely any navigational aids on my part. I would have loved to celebrate by giving her a big bag of whatever horses celebrate with…but my first pay check wouldn't come for two weeks.

The first order of business was filling our tummies. Now Lightning had no trouble. The fields were her dinner plate. I admit to sin #3 to fill mine. I had been sneaking food from the Family Dollar for some time now. Lightning waited patiently as my getaway horse while I snagged a pocketful of candy bars. Three weeks of eating mostly candy bars turned even me off to sugar but Family Dollar was sorely lacking in steak and vegetables. I longed for real food.

Fortunately, whoever was supposed to be looking out for starving thieves was somewhere in the back room, or maybe taking a leak. I had no trouble grabbing dinner and then hopping back on Lightning and clomping homeward.

I'd been watching the shrimp jumping at low tide when I got an idea. I rummaged about in the empty single wide…and no immediate fish catching apparatus came to mind. But then I spied the torn screen of the bedroom window flapping in the breeze.

It was easy to yank it out, since it was pretty decrepit and mostly detached from the window anyway. Then using the swamp reeds like thread, I wove the screen into a bowl-shaped wire net. Not to boast, but it was a pretty awesome fishing net by the time I had finished.

Next, I went hunting along the edge of the field by the road for sturdy twigs. I had two uses planned for them. One would be my fishing net handle. The second would be kindling for my fire. I had found a matchbook while rummaging through the trailer for any kind of fishing pole.

Lightning followed me, munching her dinner along the way. The sun was low in the sky and I knew I had to act fast. The shrimp stopped jumping when the sun set. I guess even shrimp need a little shut-eye.

I hurried back to the trailer with an armload of wood. One stick was just the perfect size for my fishing net handle. I attached it securely with my reed thread and headed off to go fishing. Lightning followed me, her ears perked forward and muzzle twitching with curiosity.

Almost instantly, the shrimp and little fish were tickling my ankles when I waded in the shallow water. In no time, I had collected a good sized pile of shrimp, all wiggling and springing about on the ground.

Starting my cook fire wasn't quite as easy. I used four matches before the kindling finally took hold of a flame. Next, I gathered all the shrimp back in my wire net and held them over the fire. They didn't like that very much and to tell you the truth, I felt bad for the shrimp. I asked God to forgive me for burning them alive. It didn't seem like a good way to die, but I was close to dying myself from living on Milky Ways and Snickers for the past month.

They died pretty quick, which I was glad about. And I was so famished for real food that I burned my fingers ripping off their blackened husks and then scorched my tongue shoving them in my mouth.

Man, that was a feast. A few third degree burns were nothing to complain about when compared to that fresh seafood dinner!

Lightning stood nearby the whole time, watching me. She was mighty skinny, and I wondered what she did about water. I doubted she drank the briny swamp water. Maybe at night she snuck off and found a fresh water supply.

I guess I have to admit to sin #4, now that I mentioned water. I had to steal a jug of water from the drug store. Every night, I would refill that water jug at the Kumsquat Oasis bath house. I used it to brush my teeth, and to keep my insides hydrated. But I had to steal the initial jug.

Oh, which reminds me of sin #5. I stole a toothbrush too. Please don't think badly of me. I only took what I had to in order to survive. Lord knows no one was going to keep me on as an employee if I breathed on them with a mouth that reeked like a sewer.

If you've never walked in my shoes, don't judge me. I bet you never thought about these things. Some folks just take it for granted having fresh water, or a toothbrush, or a fishing pole to catch something other than a candy bar for dinner.

I am not ever gonna take anything for granted again. 'Cause I've seen what life is like when you are all alone, and you have to take care of yourself, and no one is bustin' out of the woodwork to help you. I've been there. I know.

Lightning was a comfort. She understood. Her scrawny hide with ribs poking through was proof enough of that.

As we huddled together around the fire, and I polished off the last of that sumptuous meal, Lightning nibbled at my ear. I could tell she was trying to encourage me, and tell me I done good. I had a job, a fire, and a full belly. Things were looking up.

I stretched out on the ground, next to my fire, and thought about all the things I would buy once I had a hold of my first paycheck. I would buy a bucket so I could share water with Lightning. I'd find out what horses eat and get her some. I'd buy a plate so I could eat my shrimp like a civilized person. I couldn't think of a single other thing I needed. So I fell asleep, while Lightning stood over me.

The next day, Miracle #2 arrived. In case you lost count, Miracle #1 was Lightning. She was *bar none* the best thing that ever happened to me. I had never really had a friend before. I had acquaintances, but they knew I came from the wrong side of the tracks, and were all hoity-toity about it.

While I was sitting on the porch soaking in the morning sun, something reflecting the sun in the tall reeds right near the water glimmered in my peripheral vision. (I know. Fancy word. I warned you they popped out of me now and then.) It was way off to the edge of my property, if it were my property and if there were any borders where my property ended and the nonexistent neighbors began. Which there wasn't. But I had drawn a picture in my mind of where my white picket fence would go if I had money to throw away. Which I didn't.

Anyway, curiosity snagged me and reeled me right over to whatever it was that was sparkling in the sun. Lightning perked up, following in my footsteps.

It turned out to be a beach bike, the kind with fat tires and no gears. It was pretty rusted, but there were a few shiny spots of metal still and that had been the beacon flashing proof of this miracle of transportation. Now some of you may be wondering why God sent me a *rusty* miracle. He certainly had the power to scrub the bike clean, but beggars cannot be choosers, and I was grateful.

Walking to Better-Mart would be a far piece. Biking there would be a cinch! First I had to pull the bike out of the swampy glue it was mired in. That was much easier said than done. I wished I'd had a rope, because then I could have had Lightning help me. (I added rope to my list of things to buy with my first paycheck.)

She looked like she wanted to help me. She stood right behind me with perked ears, and even nickered once or twice, like she was encouraging me to be strong and persevere.

It took quite a bit of time, but finally, with a huge sucking sound, the fat tires wrenched free of the goo, and the bike almost knocked me over with the force of release. I surveyed my prize.

While muddy and rusty, not a single thing was broken on it. The chain was covered in slime and I imagined it would need some oiling. I rolled the bike over to the water, and spent the next hour scrubbing it with my hands. I had nothing else to scrub with.

When all the mud was off, as well as some of the skin from my hands, it was time for a test drive. Lightning put her ears back, and slashed her tail about as I straddled the bike. She clearly thought I was mounting a strange dangerous animal. She snorted when I pushed off and started wobbling over the field.

While I never owned a bike as a little kid, I had ridden one a few times. My next door neighbor took pity on me, and taught me on his bike. I must have decent balance, because in no time, I wasn't so wobbly and soon I was sprinting all over the field.

Lightning surprised me with a surge of energy and trotted behind me. We must have made quite the picture. My long tangled hair streaming behind me while I pedaled as fast as I could on that old rusty bike, and Lightning's long tangled tail streaming behind her as she trotted in my wake.

It was about the most fun I'd had in my entire life.

I rode that old bike for at least an hour. My thighs were aching and my seat was pretty sore by the end, but I was feeling like I'd died and gone to heaven.

I owned a bike.

I always wanted a bike.

When I finished riding out of sheer exhaustion, I carefully rolled the bike up the stoop and into the trailer. I paused to thank God for this miracle, just in case He was real, and feasted my eyes on my first possession of value.

Lightning neighed then, and I came back out.

"Let's go exploring," I said.

I had not yet meandered up river along the shore. For one thing, I was afraid of whatever creatures might be lurking, and for another, I was worried about someone seeing me and reporting me to Social Services.

However, now that I had Lightning, I could ride and she would protect me. My worries about other people spying me were decreasing by the day. I never saw a soul on or around the river.

I scrambled up on Lightning, and used her mane to tug her in the direction I wanted her to go. She was a mighty compliant horse, and willingly trudged along roughly in the direction I urged her.

She splashed in very shallow water, and paused to drink some. She didn't drink much. The Suwannee connects to the ocean. I knew that much. I didn't know how far the ocean was, but I can't imagine that water tasted very good. I knew it was salty, because when I washed off in it, some trickled in my mouth.

I remembered from the little education I had absorbed that the area between the ocean and the inland rivers was called an estuary. It was half fresh and half salty. I also knew that some sea creatures could exist in both. In Florida, Manatees liked the warmer water of the estuaries and fresh-water springs during the winter. In the summer, they returned to the coastal ocean.

I'd read that dolphins could live in the estuaries too. I hadn't seen dolphins or manatees yet, but I hadn't spent much time exploring. I'd been too worried about surviving. My shrimp dinner and imminent paycheck changed all of that.

It was time to investigate my world.

One of the first treasures I spied was a rope hanging from a live oak along the shore line. I imagine some kid hung it up there on a low hanging branch about a million years ago. It was pretty frayed at the bottom.

I hopped off Lightning, and clawed my way up the tree. There were some touch and go moments as I crawled out on the branch where the rope was tied.

For the record, untying an old knot that has been there since time began is not an easy feat. However, I could think of a million uses for a rope and I was not going to give up on this gift dropped right in my lap. (Or it would drop after I got the stupid knot untied.)

After several minutes and broken fingernails, I managed to loosen the knot and haul in my catch. The rope was at least twenty feet long, and heavier than you would think. I let it drop with a thud.

Lightning's head shot up when the rope plopped to the ground near her hooves. She looked up at me, with a quizzical look on her face. She shook her head, almost like she was clearing her mind of this strange image.

I shimmied back down the trunk, adding some raw patches on my legs to the ripped up sections of my fingers. It was worth it though. This was a five-star day. A bike, a rope. What other wonders of the universe might be waiting for me?

I coiled the rope around Lightning's neck, since it was too unwieldy for me to carry. She didn't seem to mind at all. We continued on our path along the water's edge, scanning the shallow water for the next surprise.

The next surprise almost knocked me off Lightning's back. There was the sound of an explosion of air, just off shore, not five feet from us, and then a huge fin surfaced.

"Shark!" I shrieked.

I don't know if Lightning knew how dangerous a shark was but she decided she wanted to check it out. She headed into the water towards the shark!

I pulled my legs up around her chest, and tried to tug on her mane to turn her around but she was ignoring me completely. She blew air out her nostrils lowering her head to the water.

"No, no!" I cried, tugging on her mane to turn her or stop her with all my strength. It was useless. The horse had a death wish.

The enormous silver shape edged closer, sensing fresh meat. I had read that sharks can smell one drop of blood ten miles away. Here I was with freshly skinned knees and fingers and way more than one drop of blood calling to the hungry shark.

The shark approached, still mostly submerged till he was within three feet of Lightning's legs. It was very shallow water. I was a little surprised he could swim in such shallow depths. Then he surfaced and air spouted out of a hole atop his head.

A dolphin!

I had never seen a dolphin outside of a book, but the friendly smiling mouth was unmistakable. As was the blowhole. Sharks are not mammals and don't breathe air.

The dolphin eyed Lightning, and then appeared to look at me. I think he must've been feasting on the ever-present shrimp and we had surprised him. When he saw me, he vanished as instantly as he had appeared. The murky water swallowed him, and I could see nothing that indicated it hadn't been a hallucination.

Lightning whinnied, and pawed at the water. What a strange reaction! It was almost as though she knew this dolphin, knew it was harmless, and wanted him to come back.

The strangest thought came to me. Did the dolphin know Lightning? Was it *me* who scared him off…not the horse? No. Impossible. *Impossible!*

Lightning continued to gaze out at the water with longing on her face, ears tipped forward, nostrils flared. We stood facing the Suwannee for several minutes, scanning the water for any break in the clear surface, any ripples indicating a huge animal swimming, any tell-tale spout of air.

The dolphin did not reappear. Lightning told me when we needed to call it a day. With a grunt, she turned and ambled slowly back to the trailer.

I slid down her side, and uncoiled the precious rope from her neck. It was a little waterlogged, and that is why it was so heavy. Must have soaked in decades of rain from the looks of it. Hopefully it would dry out now that the rainy season was over. Leastways, I hoped it was over. If it ever was.

I coiled the rope on the back bedroom floor near the window where the sun could hit it. When I came back outside, Lightning was having a snack near the water, chomping on some of the water reeds.

I sat on the porch to watch the water. Now that I knew dolphins were in it, I had something exciting to capture my attention. I peeled my eyes, shading them from the sun, and tried not to blink. Lightning sure looked like she was doing the same. She ripped some reeds from the bank and then stepped forward, hock deep in the water, chewing and watching.

There! The telltale sound of water mixing with air out a blow hole. Lightning stilled. I saw the tip of the fin surface. I could see now that the fin curved slightly. A shark fin was more straight edged. I wouldn't be fooled again.

The fin rose higher above the water as the dolphin came closer. A whole spattering of shrimp leaped from the water, and fell back like a sandstorm against the surface.

Lightning nickered, and stepped into the river, now knee deep. She shook her mane and dipped her muzzle low, almost touching the surface. Her blast of air sent small ripples across the water.

What happened next was so unbelievable that I actually rubbed my fists into my eyes. The dolphin surfaced right in front of Lightning, and then touched noses with her. I didn't dare breathe, for fear of startling one of them, or breaking the incredible image into a million pieces.

Since when do horses and dolphins commune? I could maybe understand Lightning being lonely enough to check out a dolphin…but a dolphin had a whole oceanful of friends. What would make a dolphin show any interest in a horse?

None of it made sense, and I know you think the hot sun had gotten to me and it was a mirage. I would not have believed it if I hadn't seen it myself.

The dolphin opened his mouth, and I startled. I never really noticed how many teeth a dolphin has. All you ever notice is the big friendly smile. The rows of teeth could certainly do damage! I feared for a moment that he was going to chomp Lightning's muzzle, but instead, he let out a stream of chattering sounds.

Lightning neighed, with an eerily similar staccato beat. Back and forth the two conversed, as thought they were exchanging gossip. It looked like they knew exactly what the other was saying, and they never interrupted each other.

By now, I was sure I was dreaming, and ended up on my feet somehow, mouth hanging open walking slowly towards this impossible pair of friends. I was halfway to the water when the dolphin noticed me, and in a flash of silver, was gone. It was as though he'd never been there.

I named him then and there. Flash. What else could you call him? Well, you could call him Flipper, but that was cliché. I waded into the water beside Lightning and put my hand on her withers.

How on earth had they met? How I wish she could speak English as well as she apparently spoke dolphin. This was a story I would give anything to know.

Shrimp leaped out of the water, reminding me I was getting hungry. I headed back to the trailer to get my fishing net, pondering what I had seen

Chapter Four

I watched the water 24/7 the last day before my official start day at Better-Mart. There was no further sign of Flash. I was getting a little nervous, sitting on the porch with nothing to do but look for the dolphin. It gave me time to think about what might be involved in being a cashier at Better-Mart.

What if it was something I couldn't learn or couldn't do? I had never had a job before. How would I stand being inside for eight hours a day talking to people? What if they started asking me questions? Like about my parents. Or my home. Or why I only had one set of clothes. Or if I had ever seen a dolphin make friends with a horse?

I needed a story. I needed to make sure I had it all ironed out and kept my lies nicely ordered. I was safe using my real name, and had to anyway since they had seen my social security card. I'd already told them I lived with a friend in Kumsquat Oasis. It would be a good idea to find an actual street address.

The hiring manager, who was Nancy Beam by the way, already knew my parents were no-good addicts and so I would just say they were in rehab and I was staying with friends till the precious parents got out or overdosed. Whichever came first.

What would I tell them about school? They knew I was sixteen, and they knew I dropped out. I didn't love that story though, even though it was true, because I think it marked me as an imbecile.

While usually that was my modus operandi, it might not work in this situation. I wanted to advance quickly through the dizzying heights of where I could climb in Better-Mart. I figured if I got promotions, I would get raises. It would not be wise to play the stupid card here.

So why did I drop out of school?

I pondered this while staring at the Suwannee, hoping for a fin to break the surface. No luck. It was as still and monotonous and void of excitement as usual.

Lightning grazed nearby, with no interest in the water. Maybe she knew Flash was not in the neighborhood. How she knew that, I could not imagine, but she had sure been aware when Flash was nearby the day before.

Maybe I could be a genius. Maybe I dropped out of school because I finished all my education two years early. That would impress the Better-Mart mucky mucks. The only problem was they might expect a diploma then, and I didn't have one.

Maybe I dropped out to care for my little sister. If they asked where my little sister was I would tell them she died. Of course that might reflect poorly on how well I cared for her.

There was no easy way out of it. Dropping out of high-school was a black mark against me.

The one set of clothes would be rectified as soon as I got my paycheck. I had to buy at least one more work outfit. The smock they gave all employees would help hide the fact that I wore the same shirt the first couple of weeks. Maybe no one would notice.

Day stretched into evening, and there was still no sign of Flash. I caught my supper, as usual. Much as I loved shrimp, I was getting sick of them. It was like eating Milky Ways day after day. Eventually, whatever you eat if you eat too much of it, you lose desire for it.

I think this applies to more than just food. The one thing I can't imagine this happening with is happiness. Do you think if you had too much happiness day in and day out, you would get sick of it? Would you go out looking for some sadness to break the monotony?

It was not likely I would ever find out the answer to this problem since happiness had not been an overflowing commodity in my life.

At least up to this point. I have to say, I was probably as happy as I had ever been, with Lightning, the prospect of Flash, and twenty feet of rope. It felt like I had all one could possibly want, or at least *expect* in this life.

I sat on the stoop as the sun set, having finished my shrimp. Since I didn't have a watch, I knew I had to bike to Better-Mart at the first sign of daylight in the morning. I could not be late for my first day on the job.

I added that to my growing list of essential items with my first paycheck: a watch. At least I could cross *rope* off the list.

The sun was making quite a show for my last night as an unemployed vagrant. There was every shade of red and yellow melting across the horizon. Really spectacular.

Lightning perked up, and walked to the water's edge, and at first I thought she was watching the sunset too. But then, there was a wet whoosh of air, and Flash surfaced just a few feet in front of her. I could barely see him in the waning light, but it was clearly him. Here's how I could tell. There was a little nick in his dorsal fin, right about in the middle of the underside curve. I don't know if that was a cut, or scar, or maybe dolphin fins are made that way. Like I said, he was the first dolphin I had ever seen up close.

Lightning splashed into the water that was sparkling with all those glorious colors of the setting sun, sending droplets of magenta, and coral, and bright yellow all around her legs. Flash again came right up to her, and they carried on their neighing and chattering exchange. What on earth…or on sea…could they be talking about? They were clearly talking. I may be a high school dropout, but that much was obvious.

Then, there was silence. Lightning turned and looked at me. I could not see her clearly in the waning light, but I had the strongest sense that she was beckoning me to come.

I stood up and walked slowly forward. Flash was barely moving. I couldn't see if he was watching me or not but his fin was steady in the water. I came alongside Lightning and stopped there. Then she turned back to Flash, and nickered very softly. Flash was silent. He slowly brought his face even with the surface of the water, and we gazed into each other's eyes.

I had seen pure evil before, many times in my parents' sunken eyes. I had never encountered pure gentle sweetness however. That's what I saw in the eye of the dolphin.

We stared at each other for just a flicker of a moment, and then he submerged and was gone. If it had been a test, I had no idea if I had passed or not.

Chapter Five

I decided it might be best to not take a chance changing into my work clothes in the parking lot again. So I put them on at home, and then rolled my nice new (old) bike out of the trailer.

Lightning was munching reeds as usual. She didn't even look up when I tiptoed around the corner of the trailer, rolling my bike as quietly as I could. I didn't want her to see me. She could not follow me today.

If I had to, I would tie her to the trailer, but I preferred not to. However, I didn't have to worry at all. She threw a quick look my way, but then returned to her fibrous meal. It was as though she knew she could not come with me to work.

The bike was definitely a gift from God (or random cosmic forces) but that's not to say it was perfect. The rusty chain caught on the gear teeth about every third or fourth pedal rotation with a sudden lurching clunk. It also squeaked and squealed like a stuck pig. There would be no top-secret stealth missions on this clunker!

No matter. I didn't need to be quiet or stealthy this day. I was legally and gainfully employed and determined to put my thieving days behind me. It only took me fifteen minutes to pedal to Better-Mart. I was barely sweaty when I arrived.

My first problem was hiding my bike. I added 'bike lock' to my mental list of things to buy with my first paycheck. For now, I needed to hide it where no one would find it. I suspect even if it were found, there wouldn't be many folks on the prowl for a rusty, no gear, squeaky old bike. But it was a priceless treasure to me. I hid it in the small forest just behind the Better-Mart.

Miss Beam beamed at me when I arrived. She was well named. I liked her right from the start, and not only because she hired me. She greeted me at the door and directed me to follow the signs to the cashier training session.

"Oh, and I see you rode a bike. We give employees a bike lock and numbered section for your bike."

Now that was about the most civilized thing I'd ever heard! I scratched bike lock off my mental list.

I was the only one there. I glanced at the wall clock as I slid into a chair. 7:45. Not bad for someone without a watch. Slowly other employees started trickling in. They were all way older than me. One other girl was maybe within a decade of my birthday, but all the other people looked to be at least thirty. Old as the planet!

The youngish one sat down next to me.

"Hi. I'm Lauren," she said.

"Hi. I'm Leah."

"I seen you around the Kumsquat Oasis," Lauren said.

Oh-oh. It wasn't like the KO was a sprawling city where one could get lost in the winding streets that went on for miles. She probably knew everyone who lived there. My carefully prepared lie was about to crumble.

"Do you live there?" I asked, stalling for time.

"Nope. Just visiting my dad. My parents are divorced. I live with my Mom in Elkton.

I didn't know where Elkton was but as long as it wasn't Kumsquat Oasis, my lie was safe.

"Do you live there?" she asked, "My dad is Derrick Munster."

"Staying with friends," I told her, "I don't know many of the people. I haven't been there very long."

"Where are your parents? Do they live near here?"

"Uh. No. They live… up North. They sent me here while they….um…my parents are not well."

"Join the club," she said, "Whose are?"

I smiled, thinking that was a little callous of her, but probably came out of her own less than stellar home life. I could relate.

"I mean, I'm sorry. I hope they will be ok."

"Well, they don't think so. That's why they sent me here. They didn't want me to see them die."

"Oh gosh, I'm really sorry!"

"It's ok. I've accepted it. I'm sure they'll be in a better place."

Lauren shook her head, and looked stricken. I felt a little bad for lying, but honestly, the real story was even sadder.

"I was working at McDonalds before," Lauren told me, "And then this came up and I jumped on it! How about you?"

"I wasn't working. I had to take care of my folks. In fact…" This suddenly gave me a brainstorm. I concocted the solution to my drop-out status instantly, "I had to quit school to be their full time nurse."

"Wow, that's rough."

"I stayed with them till they got so sick that they had to go to the place where old sick people go to die."

I knew there was a name for that, but couldn't come up with it for the life of me.

"Hospice?" Lauren asked.

"Yes. That's it."

"What was wrong with them? How terrible they both were so sick at the same time! Was it cancer?"

"Yes. And it was a contagious kind. That was why I had to be sent away."

I was a little worried about this last fudge, because I wasn't sure that there *was* any contagious cancer. I had always been an imaginative person, and the story was taking on a life of its own.

Fortunately, Lauren didn't question the contagious cancer line. She shook her head, with a mournful look on her face, and then decided to switch subjects after a proper period of respectful silence.

"You gonna stay with your friend for a while?"

"Till I can get my own place," I said, wishing she would stop being so nosy. The more questions she asked, the more lies I would have to remember.

Fortunately, Miss Beam came in the room and told us we were ready to start the training session. She handed out a bunch of manuals to everyone which told us all the wonders and joys of being a Better-Mart employee. I was especially happy to see that once I worked there three months, I got a 10% discount, even on some food items. And during the holiday season there was a special 20% discount day for employees.

The rest of the day was boring. Since being a Better-Mart employee is not the reason I am telling this story, I will just gloss over the slow parts, and give you the highlights.

Being a cashier is not rocket science, and even a high school dropout can learn it. It took no time for me to master how to ring up a sale. Miss Beam made a point of telling me I was a 'quick study' and would advance quickly.

We got a break halfway through the morning, and they passed out snacks. Today, we were even going to be served a special lunch to welcome us. It would be the only lunch I would get till payday, so I was really excited about that.

The rest of the afternoon was spent getting a tour of the store. If you've been to one Better-Mart, you've seen them all. They are all exactly alike. I will spare you the details.

We finished the tour and were issued our special smock and name tag. Except for Lauren, no one took much interest in me, so I didn't have to worry about marring my integrity by further lies about my present circumstances.

Now lunch was worth writing home about if I were inclined to write home. Ever. Which I was not. Since there was a sub shop right on the premises, we were served a six-inch sub with our choice of chips and a soda. Having eaten nothing but Milky Ways and Shrimp I'd murdered for the past three weeks, the sub was a blessed change of pace.

I could've eaten three, but they only offered one. I'd polished it off before Lauren had taken three bites of hers. She watched me, a quizzical look on her face.

"How do you stay so skinny eating like that?" she asked.

"I have worms," I told her.

She recoiled, and I realized I was going to need to squelch the story-teller in me.

"Just kidding," I said.

The rest of the afternoon was spent practicing more on the cash register. We also had to listen to a speech about being sensitive to those who were different or 'special' in some way and how not to make fun of them or discriminate against them. A bunch of the classmates glanced my way during this time. Which I did not appreciate.

At 4:00, we were dismissed and told to return, bright-eyed and eager to greet customers at 8 a.m. the next morning. I dashed out ahead of the crowd, so that Lauren wouldn't try to walk out with me. The last thing I needed her to see was my rusty old bike hidden in the forest.

The bike was thankfully still there. I rode it around the back of the Better-Mart and out a side alley. The other employees drove away being none the wiser.

I couldn't wait to get home and change out of my fancy duds and tell Lightning about my day. I pedaled with the bike's rusty chain screeching like an angry hawk.

Chapter Six

Lightning's head shot up the moment she heard the bike screaming my return from a mile down the road. I was not going to be able to work for the CIA unless I got quieter transportation, that's for sure. On the plus side, I don't think the CIA hired high school drop-outs anyway.

I was overjoyed because I had not been at all certain Lightning would still be there when I returned from my first day being gone all those hours. The weird thing is I think Lightning understood, and she didn't act like she had spent the day pacing or ripping her mane out in anxiety.

We had several hours of daylight left. That's the beauty of the summer. It's like God's cosmic whipped cream on the hot fudge delight of summer. I was eager to do some more exploring before my shrimp buffet. I changed quickly out of my work clothes, and clambered aboard Lightning. This time, I steered her upstream, wondering again how far the ocean was. We plodded along the water's edge.

It was not always easy to stay along the water. Sometimes it got marshy, and poor Lightning struggled to pull her hooves out of the muck. I had to turn her closer to the road that curved this way and that, roughly parallel to the river.

For about a half hour, all we saw was emptiness. Osprey flew overhead and sometimes dropped like a bomb out of the sky, and then soared back up with a fish flapping in their talons. It was amazing. Almost as effective as my shrimp basket.

We also surprised a couple of Great Blue Herons, who shrieked at us with a guttural prehistoric sound, and then flapped enormous wings and lifted into the air in slow motion. Other than that, no other creatures were stirring. I was just getting set to turn Lightning back towards home, when we rounded a corner and spied a little cottage tucked on stilts in the reeds. A long pier led from the solid ground across the marshy area to the little grey cottage. A dock that extended about twenty feet into the Suwannee was in front of it.

It was the most adorable home I had ever seen. I could not wrench my eyes away. I wanted that little hut more than I wanted anything on earth.

Lightning paused to let me take a long look at it.

I had never felt much longing for home before. Trust me, the home I'd known with my folks didn't leave much space for happy dreams of domesticity. I was content, or so I thought, with my single wide with its carpet flap door and busted out screens.

But as I gaped at the neat little grey cottage, I realized that I was not content. I wanted that cute little hut, with its steel blue shutters, matching door, and shingle roof.

As I lusted after that little house, the door swung open and a tall, lanky man popped onto the deck. He was shirtless, and wore fringed jean shorts. Probably cut them down from jeans himself, judging from the uneven edge. He looked maybe a little older than me, but not much. While I was sizing him up, he turned, and noticed us.

"Well hello!" he called.

I startled, and jumped into action, pulling on Lightning's mane to swing her around. The last thing I needed was a neighbor snooping around or knowing he even *had* a neighbor. I panicked.

Lightning, normally the epitome of an obedient steed took that moment to mutiny. She didn't budge. Not an inch.

"You from the Kumsquat Oasis?" the man asked. Not really a man. A boy. Maybe just out of high school.

I found my voice. "Yep. Staying with a friend there."

We were a good fifty feet away, and the ground was too swampy to come closer. Not that I would have. However, the boy trotted down the pier and veered towards us.

Great. A sociable type.

As he came closer, I was less aggravated. He was not ugly by a far piece. He had the most dark brown eyes I have ever seen, almost black, but his hair was nearly white it was so bleached by the sun. Or maybe chemicals. Any way about it, the contrast to his eyes was striking.

He was ripped too. I'd never seen a six-pack of abs more finely chiseled. My guess is this was the result of a personal trainer. I had to forcibly yank my eyes off those rippling muscles. He smelled like coconut suntan lotion.

"My name's Hank," he said, stopping a few feet in front of me, "I never noticed any place for a horse at Kumsquat Oasis."

"Oh I board him…someplace else."

Hank glanced at Lightning's ribs, and I think he knew I was lying. I think he knew everything I said was a lie. I don't know how I knew that. Maybe the way his dark eyes pierced into my skull.

"Is this your place?" I asked, waving a hand in the direction of the adorable cottage.

He turned to look at it, as though he'd forgotten it was there.

"Well, it's the fishing hut. I live with my folks about two miles down the river."

The fishing hut? His house must be a sight for sore eyes if this was just the fishing hut.

"Sometimes I spend the night here. It's peaceful. I'm cleaning it up for sale. My dad has to get rid of it." He glanced back at it wistfully. I think he loved it almost as much as I did. "What's your name?"

He was looking at me again with interest, but not the uncomfortable way some men do. I suspect he had his pick of ladies. The type who go for striking eyes, and abs of steel. Which I didn't. I didn't go for *any* type of man. My father and his friends had turned me off to the male species, abs of steel notwithstanding.

"You go to school here?" he asked, while my tongue tried to decide if it should be forked, or tell him my real name.

"No. I work."

Before he could ask any more questions, I finally succeeded in getting Lightning to follow my tugs on her mane and turn back down the river side path.

"I gotta get going," I said, "Nice meeting you."

Hank waved, not acting at all put off by my abrupt end to our conversation. I appreciated that.

"See ya around, I hope," he said. "If you see me at the hut, feel free to stop by. If you're lucky, I'll have some fresh gator meat."

Gator? I froze.

"Like in alligator?" I asked, swinging back around.

"Sure."

I gulped. "Do they live here…along the river?"

"Not so much this close to the ocean. Mostly they prefer further up river. Sometimes they come this way. You haven't seen them?"

I shook my head. I knew there were probably dangerous creatures all over the swamp. However, since I'd been here weeks now and hadn't seen one, I kind of dropped them out of my mind.

"They don't usually bother people," he added, probably noticing my blood draining into my toes.

"Do they taste good?" I asked.

"Like chicken." He grinned, and I figured it was a joke.

"Are they hard to kill?"

"Not when it's you or them."

"You mean you've been attacked!?"

"A few times."

I eyed him. Was he fibbing? Was it even legal to hunt alligators? He must have figured out I was dubious.

"I'm telling the truth. My dad works for the FWC…that's Florida Fish and Wildlife Conservation."

"That's not conserving them if you kill them," I pointed out.

"We're only allowed two a season," he said.

"What happened that they attacked you?"

"You don't want to get around them during nesting season. Sometimes when I help my dad we get a little too close. It wasn't a real big one. Maybe four-foot."

"How do you kill them?" I asked.

I don't know why I was asking all these questions. I sure wasn't going to try to kill an alligator, no matter how sick I got of eating shrimp. But I was fascinated by those dark eyes, and white hair, and his crazy story.

"Well, normally there are three or four of us, and we use harpoons, and special hooks…but this time, the gator was attacking my rowboat. I used a crossbow. I was lucky I got him before he smashed the boat...well....got her. It was a nesting mama."

I was having a hard time picturing an alligator as a loving mama. Frankly, given my history, I had a hard time picturing a loving mama at all. Totally outside my experience.

"Did you know that even after they are dead, their jaws can snap closed and take your head off?"

I didn't know that. It was a fact I would not have minded living another fifty years without knowing. Stuff of nightmares.

"But they are not around here?" I asked again.

"No. I didn't mean to scare you. Almost never. You'll see dolphin and manatee though. They won't hurt you."

I had run out of things to say at this point. The sun was dipping lower, and if I was going to catch my dinner, I needed to get home.

"Well, thanks for scaring the snuff out of me," I said. "I need to get going now."

"No reason to be scared," he said. "Especially on a horse. They're not going to wrangle with a horse. You never told me your name."

"Leah. And this is Lightning. On account of her color, not her speed."

"I see that," he said. "I hope you'll come visit again. Maybe I can round up some hay for your horse."

Oh yeah! Hay! That is what horses eat. I needed to find some hay and buy it with my first paycheck.

At that very moment, there was a whoosh of air, and the grey form of a dolphin surfaced just offshore. Lightning was already facing that direction, as though she knew the dolphin was about to appear.

"Flash!" Hank said.

I startled and spun around gawking.

"How did you know his name?"

"I named him. He's a buddy. Visits me a lot."

I know my mouth was hanging open like the Grand Canyon, but this was just unbelievable. It was the same dolphin I had named Flash. The nick in the dorsal fin was in the exact same place.

"See the nick in the dorsal fin?" Hank said, sending more shivers down my superstitious spine. "That's how I know it's the same dolphin. He shows up every couple of days."

Lightning nickered and ignoring the fact that I was the rider who was supposed to be doing the directing, tromped right into the Suwannee where Flash waited. They exchanged the same impossible staccato communication. Flash even lifted his head clear out of the water and smacked his long snout down a few times as though he *wanted* to splash me.

"He wants to play," Hank explained. He had walked over, knee deep in the water.

"How do you play with a dolphin?" I asked.

"Like this."

Hank dove into the water, looking more like a fish than a fish does. Flash came up right next to him, and Hank latched onto the dorsal fin. I know you think I am making this up, but I only make up lies that make sense. This was so implausible, it had to be true.

In a flash (see…it was the *only* name there could have been for that dolphin,) Flash zipped across the river with Hank bobbing along like a buoy attached to a motor boat. I would have been petrified, since I don't swim very well (or frankly…at all), but Hank was hooting with laughter.

Flash circled back to us, and Hank's hand dropped off the fin. He shook the water off his white hair in a rainbow halo of scattered droplets. Then he bellowed like a headhunter when he dangles the captive's head for all to see. (I am not really certain headhunters do that, but it seems like they would. *I* would if I were a headhunter.)

That scared Lightning, who snorted and leaped sideways. Since I had been a horse rider for all of a week, I didn't have the best reflexes. I went flying into the water.

In case you have the memory of a flea, I don't swim. So I sank like a rock to the slimy bottom of the Suwannee. That might have been the end of my pretty dismal life right then and there, except firm, smooth hands pushed me up out of the muck.

Only it wasn't hands. It was the back of a dolphin. I was too surprised, and too half-drowned to be frightened. The water wasn't over my head. If the mucky bottom had been a little firmer, I mighta been able to stand up on my own. However, Flash saved my life.

He shoved me into shallow water where even I could not drown, and then chattered to Lightning. Without time for me to thank him, he was gone, leaving a trail of bubbles in his wake.

"Oh gosh, I'm sorry," Hank said, grabbing my hand and helping me walk to the shore, "I didn't mean to scare your horse!"

I couldn't speak for a while. I had swallowed a mouthful of that putrid water and was coughing a little uncontrollably. Hank smacked my back a few times, which helped send some of the swallowed Suwannee spewing across the reeds.

Finally, I got my breath back, and leaned against Lightning.

"Well, at least you know Flash likes you," Hank said.

I wiped my watering eyes. "How do you know?"

"I've lived here my whole life. Known Flash for two years. Never seen him show the slightest interest in anyone but me. He likes your horse too. I wonder how they met."

I wondered the same thing. Warmth spread across my whole body thinking that the dolphin liked me. Had he consulted with my fellow humans, he might have come to the same conclusion they had. Fortunately, he hadn't. I felt like the queen of the world at that moment.

"I get the feeling you don't swim…" Hank said.

"No…I never got much chance to swim growing up." Now a new heat crossed over my face. A blush of shame. Sixteen and unable to swim.

"I can teach you," Hank said. He didn't even ask any questions that would force me to lie about the depressing story of my life.

"I don't know. Don't you think I am a little old to learn?"

"When did you learn to ride a horse?"

Oh-oh. This question clearly suggested Hank knew equitation was a recent acquisition.

I made the unexpected decision to be truthful.

"Last week."

Instead of making fun of me, Hank smiled in a friendly, encouraging way. His expression reminded me of Flash. He let my own words convince me.

"Well, but sitting on a horse is just balance." This was a bit of false modesty. I was actually pretty proud of how I usually stuck to Lightning's back like gravy on mashed potatoes.

"Swimming is just floating. Watch."

He flopped over onto his back, spread his arms out, and straightened his legs. The gentle current carried him away from the bank. "Nothing to it. Want to try? You're already wet."

I shrugged and moved into knee deep water. Hank swam over and stood.

"You should go a little deeper. I'll be right beside you. I won't let you go under."

I don't know why I decided to trust Hank. I guess since Flash liked him, as well as my horse, I felt a connection. Besides, if I were going to live on a floodplain, it made sense to learn how to swim.

"Ok, crouch down, hold out your arms and lean over onto your back."

For the record, this is easier said than done. I tried, but my bottom, which is heavier than my head, hit the river bottom immediately. Hank grabbed me, putting one hand under my shoulders and one under the small of my back, and then stretched me out like a plank.

"Spread your arms out!"

I did.

"Straighten your legs, and push your belly to the sky."

Again, I followed his commands.

"You're floating."

"No I'm not. You're holding me up."

Hank's hands drifted away. He was right. I was floating.

"Keep your head back!"

I didn't dare breathe. For all of you that have floated on water since you were five, like most normal human beings, this may seem like an exaggeration when I tell you I felt heaven shining down on me. I had never felt anything like it. It was like becoming a new creature, that effortless sensation of suspension on liquid clouds.

"You're a natural," Hank said.

I nodded happily and sunk like a rock.

Hank pulled me up, sputtering again. He reminded me that I had to keep my head back with my neck extended, or I would shift my center of gravity and sink.

"Try again."

I spit a few mouthfuls of stank water out of my mouth. Slowly I stretched back onto the water. This time, Hank didn't help at all. I closed my eyes and felt the gentle swells of the water rock me like I was in the arms of an angel. I almost felt like I coulda fallen asleep.

Hank brought me back to reality.

"Next time you come, I can teach you some simple things. You should know how to tread water, and then I can teach you how to move in the water."

I opened my eyes. He was smiling at me. Lightning took that occasion to plunge her muzzle against my tummy. You know what happened then. Back to guzzling salty marsh water.

"I think I have had enough for now," I said, spitting out a lungful. We both slogged back to Lightning's side.

Hank held out his clasped hands. "Leg up?"

I stuck my foot in his hands and he hoisted me up onto Lightning.

"It was nice meeting you, Leah."

I turned shy then, and clucked to Lightning to move on. She obliged, which I was happy about. Hank was real nice, and I liked him. What I didn't like was the seed of worry sprouting in my brain. If he had lived here his whole life, he would probably notice the old single wide was being occupied all of a sudden. And what if he started snooping around the Kumsquat Oasis asking for the girl who owned the horse?

I glanced at the small motor boat bobbing from the deck in front of the cottage. Which way did he go to return home? If it was my direction, I was sunk. No way could I hide Lightning.

Since I knew he was watching as I rode away, I thought it best to throw him off track. I headed to the road and turned right, away from home sweet home. After enough time had passed that I figured he wasn't watching anymore, I crossed the quiet road, and turned back towards my trailer.

Life in paradise had just gotten complicated.

Chapter Seven

I could bore you with details about my work at Better-Mart, but that is the least exciting part of my story. All you need to know is I kept to myself, and was usually so busy, that wasn't hard. There is very little worth reporting about being a Better-Mart cashier except this: if you can get a college degree as a Nuclear Physicist or something…anything.…do it. It beats standing eight hours a day ringing people out who always make the same stupid jokes and act like you must never have heard it before.

Dealing with the public was not my cup of tea. I don't want you to think I was ungrateful. I was thrilled to be bringing money in. I am just not going to pretend you want to hear the blow by blow description of monotony.

I *will* tell you about my first payday. That was eventful. Before that, life was pretty much as I have described it so far, with the added routine of biking to work each day and eight hours of dullsville in between real life.

Each late afternoon, I biked home, and Lightning was always there, always happy to see me. I never saw Hank go by in his motorboat, and I couldn't see his little cottage from the road where I biked to work. I was a little sad about that, but I didn't think it was at all a good idea to let him into my life. My secrets needed to remain secrets.

I was getting to the point where I didn't think I could eat one more shrimp dinner when I got my first paycheck. I opened a bank account right away, at a small bank across the street from Better-Mart. Then I cashed my first check. I would deposit whatever I had left when I finished my next errand.

Immediately, I returned to Better-Mart for groceries. I could only get canned stuff 'cause I had no way to keep perishables from perishing. Still, it was a feast for my taste buds who had had nothing but shrimp and Milky Ways for a month.

I wanted to spend my hard earned cash very carefully, so the only thing I bought right away was the food for that week. Juice boxes, peanut butter, bread, canned ravioli (to die for!), cheese and cracker snack packages (for the dairy content), and beef jerky strips. MMMM-mmmmmm!

Back to the bank to deposit most of the left-over money. I kept some in reserve just in case, but I figured it would not be wise to hang on to too much cash. Life with my thieving parents had taught me you cannot trust anyone, and I was easy prey in the old trailer. At the bank, I asked if there was any place they knew of where I could get hay. The teller looked at me like I had three heads.

"There's a Tractor Supply Company just past Better-Mart," she said, after looking me over like I had asked for a place to detonate an atom bomb.

"I don't want a tractor," I said, "Just hay."

"They sell all kinds of farm supplies," the teller said.

I thanked her, pocketing my new ATM card and temporary check book, and small wad of cash. It was a tiny bank, and she had seen me park my bike right in front of the bank door.

"You gonna carry a bale of hay on that bike?"

Good point.

I ignored her and headed out the door. Now my bike did have a back fender, and a small broken handlebar basket but no rack or anything I could easily strap a hay bale to. I decided I would cross that bridge when I came to it.

I hopped back on my bike and pedaled past Better-Mart, venturing to a part of my lovely new country I had not yet seen.

For the record, Tractor Supply Company is not JUST past Better-Mart like the teller promised. Maybe in a car. Not on a bike. I was just getting ready to turn around when I spied something dark lying just off the road up ahead. My curiosity got the best of me, and I pedaled on. My groceries dangled in a bag from my handlebar, too large to fit in the small basket.

I huffed and puffed along the hot dusty road to the dark object. It was a black book lying on the edge of the pavement. It looked like it had been run over a few times. I stopped and reached down to pick it up out of its dusty grave.

A Bible. It was a little dirty, and crumpled, and there were clear tire marks over Psalm 121, which is the page it was opened to. I was ecstatic.

Like I told you before, I was a voracious reader, and I had sorely missed having books around. We never owned books…don't get the wrong idea. My parents would never fork over their hard earned drug and booze money for a book. But when I was in school, I spent as much time as possible at the library.

Now the Bible would not have been my first choice. Maybe not even my tenth…but it was reading material and I was desperate. There probably was a library somewhere in Kumsquat, but I hadn't found it yet, and suspected it was further JUST down the road than the Tractor Supply Company.

I wiped the dirty tire tracks off of Psalm 121 as best I could, and read it.

I lift my eyes to the mountains-
Where does my help come from?
My help comes from the Lord,
The Maker of heaven and earth.
He will not let your foot slip-
He who watches over you will not slumber.
Indeed, He who watches over Israel
Will neither slumber nor sleep.
The Lord watches over you-
The Lord is your shade at your right hand.
The sun will not harm you by day,
Nor the moon by night.
The Lord will keep you from all harm
He will watch over your life;
The Lord will watch your coming and going
Both now and forevermore.

I surprised myself by bawling like a calf just weaned from its mama. I couldn't stop the waterfall spurting like Old Faithful out of my eyeballs. Who knows what caused that overdramatic response? I sure didn't.

All I knew was I had never been safe. No one had ever cared for me the way Psalm 121 described God as caring for the writer. No one had ever lost any sleep watching over me. No one had ever shielded any hot sun from my back. No one had ever seen my coming or going, nor worried about my safety.

I was so overcome by my pity party that I carefully laid my bike down, and sat cross-legged beside it. Then I cried for a good twenty minutes.

Fortunately, Kumsquat is not a thriving metropolis, and no one drove by and felt the need to stop and rescue me. I must have looked pitiful, knees scrunched up to my chest, arms wrapped around my shins, head leaking a flood of tears against my knee caps.

Eventually, whatever mental breakdown had caused the ruckus subsided, and I wiped away the last few tears with my grimy hands. I carefully closed the Bible and stuffed it in the bag next to the Beef Jerky strips.

Back on my bike, I continued on my way JUST past Better-Mart to the Tractor Supply Company. I should have waited a little longer because I was still heaving sobs now and then, especially when I would think about that line, *Where does my help come from.*

I guess the sheen from my tears and the glare of the sun blinded me from seeing a pothole the size of Texas in front of me. When my front tire slammed with a deafening klunk into that pit, I went flying. I landed on my hip so hard that I was sure I would set off an earthquake at a magnitude big enough to cause the destruction of Florida.

At first, the pain was so severe, I couldn't breathe. I just lay on the ground, trying to assess if it was worth even attempting to breathe. Maybe an immediate death would be the best way to deal with trauma this excruciating.

I don't know how long I lay there, wondering how a human being could endure such terrible pain, before it began slowly subsiding enough that I could stop screaming.

I didn't realize I was screaming till I stopped, by the way. That was kind of weird.

I didn't try to sit up, even as the pain ebbed to less than a dull knife slowly whittling away my bones. I didn't think I broke anything since the pain was decreasing, though slower than a snail crossing the Sahara.

I closed my eyes, with my cheek against the dirt when I heard a car coming. It screeched to a stop. A door slammed. Flip flops flapped over to me. I opened one eye when I heard a voice I knew.

"Leah!!! Are you okay!?"

It was Hank.

"I don't think so." I opened the other eye.

"Are you hurt?"

"Very."

"Can you sit up?"

"I don't know. I don't want to try right now."

"Does your back hurt, or your neck?"

I squirmed a little to check.

"No. But everything else does."

"Can you move your arms?"

I tried. I could.

"Your legs?"

I could do that too, but definitely with a lot less joy. The right one in particular, attached to the hip I'd smashed was mighty sore.

"Good. You are not paralyzed. What hurts most?"

"My dignity." I meant it too. This was pretty humiliating, lying in a heap like that.

With a groan, I pushed myself up to a sitting position. My right leg was covered in bloody scratches and holes. Nothing was gushing blood. Just oozing.

"Do you want me to help you up?" Hank asked.

I nodded, and as he put his arm around my waist, I stood. Shakily. However, despite what felt like massive bruising, nothing felt like it had detached inside from where it was supposed to be. I took a few gingerly steps.

"I don't think I broke anything."

"Let me drive you home," he said. "I can put your bike in the trunk."

I considered this. I had less than zero desire to get back on my bike at that moment. However, I wanted to bring Lightning the hay I had worked so hard to afford…and I could NOT let Hank know where I lived.

"Oh, I'll be fine. I need the exercise."

That was lame. I sure didn't need it for weight control. It really was a miracle nothing broke because my bones did not have much padding.

Hank knew this was a big fat lie but instead of calling me on it, he said, "I don't mind at all. I just have to stop at the Tractor Supply Company real quick and then could run you back to the Kumsquat Oasis."

Now was that fate or what?! I could have him drop me at the Oasis office! Dragging a bale of hay across the street would be a whole lot easier than balancing it on my head and pedaling a million miles home.

"Well…I *was* going to the Tractor Supply Company for a bale of hay. The horse boarder didn't have time to run out for some…and asked me." (Was that convincing? Not sure.) "If you could drop me at the Oasis office, she is picking it up there."

He looked at me with his eyes ever so slightly narrowed, like he was thinking this sounded a little fishy. However, instead of calling my bluff, he smiled. "Lucky I came along. How were you going to get the hay home on your bike?"

We both glanced at my bike. It appeared to be unscathed from its encounter with the humongous hole. However, my feast was dinged up a bit, though nothing appeared to have busted. My Bible was flopped open again on the ground. That gave me inspiration.

"I was hoping it would be revealed to me when I got there."

That was probably even fishier than the first lie, but it was sort of the truth. Now I was not expecting *divine* revelation, but I *was* hoping a solution would materialize when I needed it.

"Well, I guess your faith was rewarded," Hank said. "I'll get your bike. Hop in."

He gathered my dinner without a word and carefully closed the Bible and put it in the bag as well. I limped to the car and slid carefully onto the seat. Man, that right hip ached, but as long as I shifted my weight a little to the left, it was not impossible to sit.

Thump. The bike was dumped in the trunk. Hank smacked himself down beside me on the front seat.

"I go out this way at least once a week," he said. "I don't mind grabbing a bale of hay when you need it, and dropping it at the Oasis."

He didn't look at me as he said that. I didn't dare look at him. I am not a natural liar, and I felt bad for lying to Hank, who was treating me about as nice as any person had ever treated me.

"I would appreciate that," I said.

"Once I know where you live, I can just knock on your door when I'm on my way out here."

I didn't answer.

The Tractor Supply Company salesman was less trusting.

"You want just ONE bale?"

I had checked the price tag. $20 for a fifty pound bale. I sure hoped that lasted a week.

"Are you feeding goats?"

Frankly, I did not think what I did with my hay bale was any of his business. Since Hank was not with me at the moment, but off getting the tractor part he needed, I decided to have fun with the salesman.

"Well actually, I am feeding an alligator."

"Alligators don't eat hay."

"That's why I only need one bale."

The man peered at me, but rang up the charge. I hoisted the heavy bale, with difficulty, and pain went shooting through my right hip. Maybe something *was* detached.

"Ouch!" I crumpled and dropped the bale.

Hank swooped in.

"Let me help you." He lifted that heavy bale like it was a piece of cheesecake, and carried it on one shoulder to his car. He heaved it in the back seat and then clapped the chaff off his hands.

"There is no way you would get that bale home on a bike," he said.

I hated to admit it, but he was right. I had to come up with a new plan, or this feast for Lightning would be the last she'd ever have. Then I noticed a sign on the door of the Tractor Supply Company. *We Deliver.* This was good news, and I would be sure to check into that.

Hank ran back in the store to pay for his tractor part, while I wondered how I could find out how much hay a horse normally eats each day. It didn't matter. I could not shell out more than a bale a week for my horse. I would ration. She had lived this long without any hay at all.

As he drove, Hank chattered about the work he'd been doing preparing the fishing cottage for sale. My heart ached more than my hip hearing that. What I would give to be able to live in that cottage, but of course that was gonna happen right after the moon turned into swiss cheese and abolished world hunger.

"How much will you sell it for?" I asked, totally against my desire to speak of it. Why break my heart when there was no way it was $350 which is all I had left from my two weeks of work at Better-Mart?

"I'm not sure. Dad seems to think we can get $180."

$180! I had that much! And then I'd even have enough for hay each week.

"I told him no way was someone gonna pay $180 thousand for a one bedroom hut on a floodplain. I think he will be lucky to get $100."

Oh. I was sure glad I hadn't spoken. I know what you are thinking. For a sixteen-year-old, I had the brains of a jellyfish. Try living my life and then judge me.

"I told him he should just rent it to fishermen on vacation."

I nodded.

We were at the Kumsquat Oasis in no time. Cars are a whole lot more efficient than bicycles. Or horses.

He stopped at the office, pulled out the hay bale, and my bike. Then he handed me my bag of groceries.

"So when will the farm owner be coming?" he asked, looking around.

"Oh soon. Any minute."

"Well, I can make it a regular Thursday run to the TSC. Where do you live?"

How was I going to wiggle out of this one? He looked around, waiting for me to point out the one of three streets I might live on.

At that moment, there was a familiar neigh, and who should be traipsing across the street but Lightning. We both swung around to see her clip-clopping across the quiet road.

I peeked at Hank. The need to come up with a convincing story was getting more dicey by the second.

"Sometimes when I am at work, the farm ties her over by the river. She likes to stand in the water."

Hank looked at me.

"By the old motor home?" he asked.

I nodded.

He knew.

"Well, let's bring the hay over there. If that's where she spends her days, maybe it would be best. I bet I could rustle up a tarp in my trunk you can throw over it to keep the rain off."

I nodded, not daring to speak. He knew I'd been lying. He knew I lived in the abandoned trailer. If he told his dad, the gig was up. I would be reported and social services would swoop down on me like a turkey vulture on road kill.

I wheeled my bike behind him. He hauled the bale back onto his shoulder and traipsed off towards the Suwannee. Lightning stayed close on his heels, sniffing the bale. I was doleful. As soon as he saw the clothesline, the firepit, the shrimp fishing basket, any pretense that I wasn't living there was over.

When we reached the trailer, he dropped the bale down. Instantly Lightning began nibbling at the edge.

"Maybe put it in the trailer so she doesn't eat it all in one sitting," I said.

He hefted it back to his shoulder, to Lightning's dismay and I preceded him up the small creaky stoop. I held back the carpet piece. He walked in and neatly laid the bale down against a wall.

Then he looked around.

"How long you been living here?" he asked.

"I don't know. About a month," I said, looking at the floor.

"How old are you?"

I didn't want to answer, but I was powerless now. There was no place to run. No other place to hide. My only hope was the truth I decided.

"I'm sixteen. My parents are addicts and were glad to get rid of me. When I work up enough savings, I will get a place, but right now, I'm not hurting nobody, and no one lives here. Please don't tell on me. Don't tell your father. If anyone knows they'll take Lightning, and they'll take me."

Hank didn't speak. He stared at me, as though working through a calculus problem. Finally, he asked, "What do you do about water?"

"I go to the Oasis. I use their washroom to shower and fill my water jug. Sometimes I wash off in the river."

"How have you been cooking?"

"I catch shrimp and cook over the firepit. I have enough money to get a Coleman stove now, with my Better-Mart discount."

"What will you do when it gets cold?"

"It's Florida," I reminded him.

"Nights in the winter can be freezing," he said, "Even here."

"Not often. I will have enough money to buy a coat by then."

"If my father, or anyone, sees you, they will report you."

"No one comes by here...ever... the only person I ever see is Flash, and he's not a person." I smiled a little weakly. "Though I haven't seen him since that time with you."

The carpet flap suddenly pushed into the room. A muzzle lifted beneath it.

"Oh! Lightning is waiting for her treat!" I pulled one string off the hay bale and lifted one rectangular section of hay. Hank followed me out the doorway.

Lightning was beside herself with joy as she dived into the hay.

"I wonder how she has survived," Hank said.

"I wondered too. She seems to live on the river reeds and grass. She even drinks the water, though I bet she has some fresh water supply somewhere I don't know about."

"There are plenty of ponds," Hank said. "So how did you end up with her?"

"She found me. She showed up the first day I was here. It was almost like she was waiting for me."

Hank sighed, and blew out a lungful of confusion.

"I don't think it is a good idea, what you are doing. There are a million ways you could be hurt out here."

"There are a million ways I *was* hurt out there," I said, tilting my chin at the world on the other side of the street.

"I won't tell...for now. But you have to let me help you."

"You can bring the hay," I said.

"We need to get you electricity and water."

"We can't. No one can know I'm here."

"I can do some snooping," he said. "With my Dad's job, I'm pretty sure I can find out who owns this. At some point, they must have had services."

"You won't tell him?"

"No, I can be pretty sneaky when I want to be."

He picked up the bag of groceries I'd put beside the bike. Without a word, he carried it into the trailer and slowly pulled each item from the bag placing it on the counter in a row. The Bible was at the end of the lineup.

"You some sort of religious nut?" he asked. "I don't mean that in a bad way, 'cause I sort of am."

"No. I found it. Right before I crashed my bike."

Hank looked over my food stash.

"No calcium."

"Cheese crackers," I said pointing to the snack packages.

"No vitamin C. You'll get scurvy."

"Juice packs." I held one up and read the label, "100 % daily recommended level of vitamin C."

"Green vegetables?"

I looked over the lineup. "Nope. Lucky me!"

He turned from assessing the nutritional value of my groceries, and pushed the carpet flap so it swung back and forth.

"I can put a door on this. Won't be a new one, but we just switched out an old screen door back home."

I must have looked happy, because he said, "Though I like how the carpet flap lets in the river breeze. Nice splash of color too."

"I wouldn't mind a door," I said.

"I can swing by tomorrow."

"I'll be at work all day," I said, "But Lightning will let you in."

Hank glanced at his watch.

"My folks will be looking for me now," he said. "If you are going to stay, we need to make this safe. I won't say anything as long as you will let me help you."

I thought of Psalm 121. No one had ever wanted to help me. No one had ever cared what happened to me. I was burning to ask, *why did he?*

"Thanks," I said instead.

Chapter Eight

In case anyone has ever told you differently, the next day after smashing your hip full force onto pavement and pebbles is NOT FUN.

I made it through the day of work, but it was not easy. I eyed the Coleman stove again in the Better-Mart camping department. $46 for the two burner model. Of course, I'd have to buy the propane fuel too. $11 for 14 ounces. I had no idea how much I would need. However, I decided that shelling out $60 to be able to cook a meal was a steal. I threw in a small camp stove pot for another $4. Forking over another ten dollars for two t-shirts with pretty designs on them was a no-brainer. I figured they would be suitable for work and play shirts. I also bought $10 of toiletries. You don't need to know about them.

It hurt to bike, but with my new purchases clanging, I made it safely back to the trailer. You won't believe what greeted my eyes! A brand new screen door had replaced the carpet flap. A glass section was slid down so the wind could blow through the screen. I felt like I had died and gone to heaven.

A door, new shirts, and a stove all on the same day.

Hank was not there. I felt a whoosh of disappointment as I opened my new door to see the trailer was empty. He had done his work and not even hung around for a thank you.

Now to be perfectly accurate, the door was not new. There was a significant rusty dent in the middle bottom portion. Someone had kicked that door hard. Some of the rubber stuff that holds the screen snug was peeling away, but only a little. To me, it was better than Christmas!

I set my new stove and propane on the counter with the little pot, and stood there for several minutes looking at it. Just think! I could cook soup, or heat up my ravioli. The possibilities were endless.

A shrill neigh blasted through my new screen door. I had to rip my eyes of my new things. Lightning was impatient. For one thing, she had a great memory and knew the hay bale was in the trailer. I'd given her one section in the morning. Now I pulled off another rectangle of hay, and headed out the door with it.

She gobbled it down while I sat on the stoop, gazing out at the Suwannee. It was a hot day, but a cool breeze lifted off the river and made its lazy way across the tops of the reeds smack dab into my cheeks. It brought with it the pungent scent of sea life and swamp gas.

I actually liked it. When I first arrived weeks ago, the smell was overpowering, and I'd hated it. But now it smelled of home.

The sun was still quite high in the sky, though it was late afternoon. The water sparkled and danced in the sun. I was half asleep from the soothing breeze and warm sun, when I spied a fisherman through my half-mast eyes.

He was in the middle of the river and didn't notice me. His boat barely made a sound, just a tiny motor humming. He didn't have a fishing pole, but had a sack in his hand. Curious, I leaned forward. What was in that sack?

With a guilty look right and left, the fisherman flung the sack overboard. I heard a yelp, and knew what was in that sack. As soon as the splash rebounded to the sky, the motor roared to life and the boat disappeared around the next bend.

Frantically, I grabbed Lightning. I don't know what I thought she could do, but I had to try to save the puppy that I knew was in the sack. I pulled myself onto her back and steered her to the water. I couldn't swim, and knew I would drown as surely as the puppy if I tried. I kicked her sides, urging her forward into the water.

She obliged but only for a few feet. She didn't know about the puppy and saw no good reason to swim out into the river.

"Go, go!" I cried, to no avail.

As I stared powerless at the gleaming water, the sack suddenly bobbed to the surface. The pup inside was squirming. Could that have made it rise?

A split second later, I saw what made it rise. Flash's unmistakable fin surfaced just beside the sack. The dolphin had the long tied end of the burlap in his mouth.

Now Lightning took interest. She nickered, and pawed at the water. It looked like she was telling Flash to bring it here. Flash skimmed through the water as I tumbled off of Lightning's back. He came right up to me, and deposited the sack in my hands.

I untied the wet knot with some trouble, holding the bag out of the water. The puppy was silent, and I feared I was too late. Finally, the knot loosened and slipped open. I peeled the bag away to reveal a little brown hound, its eyes closed, limp in my arms. Dashing to the shore, I put the little dead body on the ground and pushed gently on its distended stomach.

A mess of putrid water flew out of him, and then he started coughing, puking up more swamp water. He sneezed and sputtered and shook all over. His eyes popped open.

It was love at first sight. For both of us. I had always wanted a puppy, but of course my parents had squashed that idea like a cockroach. It was hard to tell what kind he was, on account of he had just recovered from drowning, and he was soaking wet. Besides that, he was young. He was a golden brown with triangular ears that looked like they wanted to stand up, but then flopped over at the tip. He had a darker streak down his back, and a curved tail. His paws were small, like he wasn't going to grow up to be a Saint Bernard or German Shepherd.

Lightning lowered her head, and blew a blast of warm air on him, sniffing him. He shook himself, sending a spray of water all over her muzzle. Then Flash smacked his snout on the water and chittered at us. I think he wanted to be introduced. After all, he had saved the poor little dog.

For the first time it struck me how odd that was. Since when did dolphins rescue drowned puppies? It had been two weeks since I had seen Flash. How had he miraculously appeared at just the right moment? Besides all that totally unbelievable sequence of events, how had he known we were there? He couldn't have untied the bag himself. He instantly brought the pup right to me, as if he knew I was right there and that I could help.

The puppy now scampered to his feet, and the first thing he did was race to the water and bark at the dolphin. Flash circled coming as close as he could in the shallow water, raising an eye above the surface so he could see the dog.

You would think a little puppy would be terrified of a big sea creature like that, but he didn't seem to be. Not at all. He barked and growled, and wagged his soaking wet tail.

With a flip of his tail, Flash submerged and was gone. I guess he decided the puppy was safe and he had to get back to whatever it is that dolphins do all day when they are not rescuing puppies.

The pup barked a few more times, then remembered us. Lurching out of the water, he zipped in bounds across the muddy shore and landed in my lap.

He leaped at my chin, slathering me in swamp smelling puppy licks, and then zipped in a big circle around Lightning, barking and bounding.

That's when I named him Zippy. I never saw so much energy in one tiny creature! I would keep him, of course. Somehow. The immediate problem was that my new pet would need a collar, and food. I could share my beef jerky and ravioli tonight. I still had plenty of money left. The collar would have to wait for the morning. But that presented a new problem.

I couldn't tie him outside without a collar. But if I left him inside while I was at work, my pristine trailer would become a latrine. There was no question I was keeping him. I had to. But I hadn't had time to consider all the results of my heroics before emptying his lungs of water.

This is the way life is sometimes. You do the right thing and then you are left with a whole mess of unintended consequences. If I were drawing up the plans for the world, I would make a special provision for do-gooders. They would always get money and supplies instantly floating down from Heaven as soon as the good deed was done.

Of course, maybe then it wasn't really a good deed. Maybe then it was just selfish on account of the payback. Somehow, this good deed felt more virtuous because it put me in a pickle.

I laughed watching little Zippy race all over my yard like he was a greyhound. I think he was showing me how glad he was to be alive. It was pretty amazing how quickly he rebounded from being almost dead.

I would tell Hank first thing that he needed to teach me to swim. I didn't want to be at the mercy of the water ever again.

After every lap, Zippy catapulted back onto my thighs, took a swipe at my face with his tongue, and then darted away. Then he did the funniest thing. He started doing figure eights between Lightning's hooves. When Lightning lowered her neck to get a closer look, Zippy paused and licked her muzzle.

Lightning recoiled, and Zippy made a getaway towards the reeds at the edge of my yard. The chase was on. Lightning whinnied and trotted after the wild pup. I hadn't laughed so hard in my entire life.

Who would have thought such a close brush with death could end up in so much joy? He circled the yard at least forty times, and then finally threw himself on my lap and fell immediately asleep.

Lightning gave up the game after the fourth lap. She was munching the few leftover wisps of hay from her dinner.

I could not believe how radically my life had improved in just a month. I had my own home (at least squatter's rights to it), money in the bank, a larder filled with cans, and three unusual friends. Four if you counted Hank.

The puppy snored in my lap, Lightning stood nearby, head low enough that I could feel the gentle exhale as she took a nap herself. I gazed out at the Suwannee, hoping to catch a glimpse of Flash.

This time, I was not disappointed. There was an explosion of shrimp leaping in the air, and then the sleek dolphin catapulting clear out of the water. He smacked back down with an enormous splash. I don't know if this was his fishing technique, or if he was just having fun. It sure looked like fun!

Lightning opened her eyes, and trotted to the water's edge. Then she neighed. She was calling to him. Telltale bubbles in the shallow water outlined his path and he glided up close to the bank. He lifted his smiling face out of the water. Lightning nuzzled him, and nickered. He answered with a series of clicks and high pitched whines.

That woke Zippy up. His head sprang out of my lap, ears instantly perked towards the source of the chatter. With an acrobatic leap, he was off my lap and raced right into the water.

Fortunately, without a sack constraining him, he seemed to know how to swim by instinct. That sparked my latent courage. If a nearly drowned puppy could doggy paddle, maybe so could I.

I approached slowly, so I wouldn't scare Flash off. He didn't act like he was worried about me anymore at all. He swam in a slow circle near shore, almost as though he were waiting for me to get in.

I admit I was nervous. Dolphins are BIG. They may have nice smiles, but they still outweigh me by at least five times. Flash may have sensed my anxiety…I hear dolphins have some sort of extra-sensory perception. I read some stories back in the days when I had a library at my beck and call. There are lots of stories of dolphins saving people from drowning.

There are also less endearing stories of dolphins attacking people, though that doesn't seem to happen often. Dolphins can kill sharks so it would be wise to treat them with respect. However, Flash backed off when I came in the water like he understood I was jittery. I leaned over onto all fours, deep enough that my chin scraped the water, and then tried to move all my limbs just like Zippy was. I wasn't really deep enough to sink very far, but since I could bounce off from the river bed, it wasn't really learning to swim. More like learning to bob.

Flash mimicked me. He floated parallel to me about ten feet out. As I bobbed on a path to the left, he glided left. As I bobbed back in the other direction, so did he. It was almost like he was playing.

Zippy had worn himself out, and now sat on the shore, barking at me with his tiny sharp bark. I was getting pretty good at bobbing and propelling myself a few feet before touching down. So I moved into deeper water. If I sunk here, I would definitely get my nose wet.

I paddled as fast as my legs and arms could go, but never made it more than a foot or two before I started to go under. Flash was creeping a little closer. Every so often he would raise his snout and head out of the water, and make mewing and clicking sounds.

"Ehehehehehehe," he said.

As I flipped my arms and legs in the water, I replied. "Ehehehehehehehеh!"

This got him all excited. I had no idea what I just said to him, but whatever it was, it made him sprint off to the middle of the river and then come streaming back to me like a torpedo. I was sure he was going to ram me when he veered at the last moment.

That made Lightning excited too, and she whinnied and stamped her hoof in the water. We were all making a ruckus – Lightning whinnying, Zippy barking, Flash splashing, and me chattering, "Eheheheheh!"

I was so distracted by all our foreign languages melding as one that I forgot about worrying about staying afloat. As soon as I stopped worrying, instincts musta kicked in, 'cause while we all gabbed away as though we knew what each other was saying, I was swimming!

Now I probably would not have won any Olympic medal, even if doggy paddling was an Olympic sport. Still. I was super impressed with myself. I paddled out towards Flash, who moved further away. Flash was the one in control, no doubt. If I were to approach him, it would be on his terms.

Noticing that the river got deep fast, I paddled back towards shore. As soon as I turned, so did Flash. He still remained ten feet or so away, but he was parallel with me, following me stroke for stroke.

I could see why Zippy had given up so quickly. Doggy paddling is way more exertion than you would think. I almost didn't make it back to the mucky shallows before my lungs were ready to collapse.

Heaving huge gasps of air, I dragged myself onto shore, and flopped over next to Zippy. He took that as an invitation to crawl all over my defenseless face and start shredding my cheeks with his sharp little nails. By the time I removed the puppy from my face, Flash had disappeared. Just like that. In a flash. No pause to wave a fin toodle-oo.

I didn't blame him. Saying goodbye was never big on my list either. For me it was because most of the time, every fiber of my being was wondering and plotting how to escape. Saying goodbye would give it all away.

But on the rare occasion that I departed from someone I actually *wanted* to be around, saying goodbye only reminded me of how empty my life was. Goodbyes were closed doors.

I still wished Flash had hung around a while longer. Not only had I never had a real friend, I had never felt a part of a group. Funny that my first time being accepted involved a fin, hooves, and furry ears. It didn't matter. It felt great, this sense of belonging.

Chapter Nine

I had one inspiration, while sitting in the sun drying off. Maybe I could build some sort of temporary enclosure for Zippy. I had never looked under the mobile home, since it was so weed-covered all around it. Who knew what magnitude of creepy, crawly, deadly things lurked in those weeds?

However, the lattice pieces that covered the underside of the raised trailer could possibly be ripped off and hooked together to form a fence of sorts. I wouldn't need all of them. I imagine if there was an owner somewhere, this would count as destruction of property. I found myself (again) with the un-charitable hope that the owner was dead.

First I found a big stick, and started whacking at the weeds all around the perimeter. I hoped that would drive out any dangerous creatures. Not a thing stirred which bloated my courage a bit.

While hammering at the weeds, I clunked on a post and metal box. It had been completely hidden by the weeds. A small post about a foot high was topped by a grey metal box with a latched door. A whole bunch of thick wires ran from the box down to the ground.

Curious, I opened the little door.

It was some sort of electrical box. There were a bunch of switches and on the top, a very large switch. A piece of masking tape was by that, with the faded words: Main Power.

An electrical box! This was almost as exciting as finding a horse, dolphin, and puppy. Was this trailer hooked up for electricity? With mounting excitement, I followed the wires that ran a short distance to the underside of the trailer and disappeared.

The potential for electricity opened a whole new world for me. If I could get electricity, I could have a refrigerator. I was not one to complain, but canned food leaves a lot to be desired. If I could have some fresh food now and then, I don't even know what ecstasy that could generate!

While contemplating how to turn the electricity on without anyone knowing I was here, I ripped off four sections of the lattice. It was not very hard. Whoever had installed the lattice was a lazy carpenter. Only two or three nails held the lattice in place.

Since I had my long piece of rope, I had no trouble tying the four pieces into a sturdy square playpen. It would never have contained a grown dog, but would be plenty strong enough to keep little Zippy in place. I dragged the enclosure to the back right corner of the trailer. That section was almost always in shade. I could leave Zippy with some water in his little pen, and go to work without having to worry about my home becoming a litter box.

By now, the sun was thinking about setting. I opened my can of ravioli and cut up a few beef jerky strips to go with it. Then I fired up my new Coleman stove. It took a few times before I got the knack of it, but soon, my feast was bubbling away in my new pan. Unfortunately, the only thing I had to use as a plate was the juice box. After downing the 'apple-grape delight', I cut the juice box in half. I filled one side with water from my one jug, and filled the other side with some of the ravioli.

While preparing this feast, I made sure my new door was securely latched, and closed the door to the bathroom and bedroom. Zippy could now explore his new digs while mostly in my sight. He did a little sniffing, but mostly he prowled under my feet. I think he was hungry, and beef jerky ravioli was pretty tempting.

So that Lightning wouldn't feel left out, when the grub was done, I carried it all outside. I set Zippy's food and water down first. He lit into it like the world was gonna end in three seconds, and he didn't want to go to eternity hungry.

While he gobbled his food, I broke off a segment of hay for Lightning. Tossing that near Zippy, I finally grabbed the hot pot and my one spoon. Settling on the front stoop, I was filled with *serenity.*

That is a GREAT word, and one I don't think I had ever had the occasion to use before in my life. There were lots of sounds of slurping, and munching, while the sun slowly dipped behind some live oak trees lining the Suwannee. The sky was just beauteous – with all kinds of shades of red and orange shooting up from the horizon. My personal fireworks show.

Now that our tummies were all filled, I could ponder the electrical box. It was clear, this trailer once had power. I didn't dare flick the *on* switch yet. What I knew about electricity was even less than I knew about swimming, but I did know that I could electrocute myself fiddling with it.

In fact, maybe that's what happened with the owner of this place. It was certainly in pretty shabby shape, but it kept the rain off and the snakes out. Why had the owner deserted it…and where was the owner? I hoped his electrocuted body wasn't decomposing underneath the trailer.

I didn't know how to begin to find out who owned this place. If I started asking questions, I raised suspicion, and people might start putting two and two together.

The only person I thought maybe I could trust was Hank. After work tomorrow, I would bike to the fishing hut. Maybe I'd be lucky and he would be there. Maybe he would know how to hook up the electricity without electrocuting himself, or letting anyone who might care know that I was habitating in the trailer.

I let Zippy sleep on the couch with me that night. He snuggled in close, and his little puppy breath washed over me in warm bursts of air about every three seconds. It was so comforting that I almost didn't get out of bed on time to make it to Better-Mart without being late.

I had to race around like a tornado, getting breakfast for Zippy and Lightning. I would eat at work. I took the two juice box halves, filled one with water from my jug and the other with the last beef jerky strips. I put them both, along with Zippy, in the new lattice playpen.

Lightning relocated next to the playpen when Zippy started whining. As soon as I straddled my bike, Zippy set to mournful wailing, like someone was cutting off his tail. I had to force myself to peddle away. Someone had to earn money here, and Lightning didn't have any employable skills I could discern.

Lightning reached her muzzle through the lattice holes, though she couldn't fit her entire nose in. She wiggled a piece of it at the puppy. Zippy nuzzled against her, and quieted. Lightning was a wonderful mother.

Work hours passed as slowly as a glacier. I was definitely not cut out for the nine to five gig. I decided I was also not cut out for dealing with the public. If I didn't need the job so badly, there is zero doubt that I would have told the lady who asked me if Better-Mart only employed stupid people, "No, but we *do* only allow stupid people to shop here." I didn't say it…out loud. I just told her, "I am not sure. Let me ask someone who might be able to understand your question."

While I was on my lunch break, I priced mini-fridges. The cheapest was only $70. It went on my list. As soon as I had juice running through my home, I was buying it.

Passing by the electronics section on my way to pet products, I saw a computer. It was only $200. I didn't know they came that cheap. I filed that info away in the back of my brain.

You may wonder what a high school dropout, living in a single-wide, and barely making enough to survive would want with a computer. This is TOP SECRET so don't go blabbing it to every Tom, Dick, and Harry. I had this secret desire to write a book. I never told anyone, mostly because I was too busy running away from drunken parents or parole officers. But now that I was on the road to respectability and realizing I was not cut out for full time work at Better-Mart, I had a dream of writing a New York Times bestseller and retiring. If I had a computer, I could work on my novel. It would be based on my life since people love reading depressing stories that make them feel better about their own wretched lives.

Only I would give mine a happy ending. No matter how it really ended.

I also noticed little phones that you could get for $20 with prepaid minutes. I had no one I wanted to talk to. Having no friends is the best way to reduce your phone bill, in case you need a cost saving tip. However, it made sense to have one in case of an emergency. Like if the Suwannee flooded and I needed to call the Coast Guard to come rescue me.

When the never ending day at work finally ended, I bought the Tracfone, a dog collar and leash, two dog bowls, and a small bag of puppy chow. On a whim, I bought a ten dollar backpack. It was a luxury, but with all the carting of goods back and forth on my bike, it made sense. I stuffed my purchases in my new backpack, and pedaled home.

Zippy was beside himself with joy when he saw me. He raced around the dog pen yipping the whole time. When I lifted him out, he slathered me with dog spit, his little tail slashing my arms a mile a minute.

Lightning nickered, and nuzzled me. I noticed the grass and reeds around the dog pen were mowed. By horse teeth. Lightning had hung out near Zippy all day. I was as proud as any mother whose siblings get along.

While Zippy scampered at my feet, I poured a little puppy chow in his new bowl, and filled the other bowl with water. He lit into that puppy chow like it was Lobster Newburg. For the record, I have no idea what Lobster Newburg is, but my mom used to set my peanut butter sandwich in front of me and remind me not to be complaining it "ain't no Lobster Newburg." I assume Lobster Newburg is some delicacy that people with drug addicts for providers are not likely to encounter on a regular basis.

I didn't have to warn Zippy not to complain though. He finished his meal before a mosquito met an untimely death on my arm. I brought him inside while I changed out of my Better-Mart duds. Lightning stood at the door, looking in, like she wanted to come in too. I didn't let her.

I was just getting set to put Zippy in his pen, and head over to see if I could find Hank, when who should come waltzing up my swampland but Hank himself!

"Hi neighbor!" he said, "I was working on the cottage and wanted to see how you liked your new door."

"It's the best door I ever had," I said. "Thanks."

At this point, Zippy squirmed out of my arms and catapulted over to Hank.

"Well now. You've accumulated another pet," he said, kneeling to greet the wild waggling puppy.

"Flash brought him to me," I said.

Hank looked up with interest, cocking an eyebrow at me like he didn't quite believe me. "Flash brought him?"

"Some fisherman dumped him overboard in a bag. Flash hauled him over to me."

Hank's mouth popped open, and he squinched his eyebrows together, like he was examining a truth meter over my head.

"It's true," I said. "I wouldn't a believed it except I was there."

I am not sure Hank believed me, but he just chuckled shaking his head. "You ought to write a book!"

That took me by surprise since those had been my very thoughts while eyeing the computer at Better-Mart.

"No one will believe it," I said.

"They don't have to believe it. Just have to enjoy it, and it's a good story, even if it isn't true."

"But it is," I said, a little angrily.

He nodded. "Flash is a smart dolphin. I wonder sometimes if he was trained since he's so friendly with people. Maybe he escaped from SeaWorld."

We would never know, but I doubted it. It's not like Sea World connects to the Suwannee, and smart as he was, I couldn't see how Flash could travel overland.

"I found something while building Zippy a little pen."

Hank followed my pointing finger, and noticed the enclosure I'd made.

"You made that?" He sounded impressed.

"Yeah. I didn't want Zippy running away."

"Good name." Hank and I watched Zippy racing to the water and then circling back to us like his tail was on fire. "What did you find?"

"An electrical box. Over there."

We walked together to the small box on the post and I opened the little metal door.

"Well. Lucky you. You just have to call the power company to turn on the power."

"And then be arrested for trespassing," I added.

"There is that."

We both stared at the power box.

"I can ask around," Hank said, "Find out who owns this place. If anyone. See if they'd rent it."

"I don't know if I can afford rent," I said.

"For this dump? You work full time. I can't imagine it's much. If anyone owns it at all. My guess is the Kumsquat Oasis might've rented it. There was talk a few years back of them wanting to buy this plot of land, but then it flooded bad once, and that was the end of that."

"If they start snooping around they'll know I'm here."

"My Dad will know who owns the land. Or he can find out."

I know I looked worried. A single wide trailer without power or water on a flood plain next to a smelly swamp might not sound like much to you…but it was the first home I had ever lived in where I felt an atom of happiness.

"I will offer to rent it myself. Fix it up for whoever owns it. It's what I do for a living while earning enough money for college. No one will question that. You can just pay me the rent."

I didn't dare look at him. I felt nibbles of hope. A real home that I could legitimately stay in? It sounded too good to be true. Why would he do this for a total stranger?

"If there's electrical hook up, someone lived here once. There is probably water hook up too."

I gasped. I hadn't thought of that. Electricity *and* water?! It was like leaping a thousand years out of the Stone Age in one day. We both began slashing at the tall reeds and in no time, Hank yelled, "Bingo! Here's the water pipe into the trailer."

He was peering under the dark far corner of the mobile home. It would sure be nice having a working shower and toilet…not to mention running water in a sink.

You may have noticed I didn't mention up to this point how I managed without a toilet for three weeks. Let's just say that there are more pleasant things to discuss…like World War 3 or botulism. You don't need the details. Just know it wasn't as fun as you might think. Mostly, I dashed over to the Kumsquat Oasis bathhouse.

"We'd need to replace your screens. It must be mighty hot in there with your windows closed."

That was true. I had the advantage of the one big live oak tree that blocked the sun for most of the day. In the late afternoon the sun nibbled under the shade, and I always left the door open.

"With electricity you could get a fan," he said.

"How much do you think rent would be?"

He shrugged. "Not many people would want to live in an unairconditioned rusty old mobile home in a Florida summer. I will nose around tomorrow and see what I can find out. There's a utility assistance program that helps low income people with water and electricity. Pretty sure you would qualify."

Good to know. I may not qualify for much in life, but I had low income in spades!

"The other reason I came by was to see if you wanted another swim lesson."

"Oh, Zippy taught me yesterday." I smiled at him. He looked almost as dubious as when I told him Flash saved the drowning puppy.

"Well," I added, "Flash helped."

"Of course he did."

"I wouldn't mind a few pointers."

"Let's do it."

Zippy galloped beside us as we headed to the water, weaving in and out between our ankles.

"How old do you have to be to rent here?" I asked.

Hank pulled off his shirt and tossed it on the shore. Zippy instantly snatched it and almost dashed away before Hank lunged for him and retrieved it, *almost* none the worse for wear.

"He *is* zippy," Hank said, hanging the shirt on one of the oak tree limbs. "18 is the legal age. I can rent. I'm 19."

He stepped into the water, and then dived into the shallow water. This is not smart. I know because I had a classmate who did that in a pool and broke his neck. He ended up in a wheelchair.

"You shouldn't do that," I told Hank when he surfaced.

He didn't surface for a long enough time that I worried he had gone the way of my classmate. When he did pop back up, he was way out in the deeper part of the river.

"*You* shouldn't do that," Hank agreed.

"Teachers should be good examples to their students."

"OK. Agreed. Watch this, student."

He glided through the water like a shark. His arms lifted in and out gracefully while his legs flutter kicked behind him. I couldn't get over how beautiful he looked, skimming over the surface. It looked effortless.

He swam back towards me, and then stood in knee deep water.

"Watch. Your arms move like this, while you turn your head like this." He demonstrated. "Now you do it. Just get in knee deep water and crouch down. Don't try to float or swim yet. Just do the arm and head movements."

This may sound easy. People often use the word 'just' to make it seem like any fool could do it. I am here to tell you that it is easier said than done. I swallowed a barrelful of water trying to coordinate head and arm movements.

"Maybe I should stick to doggy paddling," I said, coughing up putrid, salty swamp water.

"Here. I will hold your body up. Just do the arm movements and keep your head out of the water."

He didn't give me a choice. He grabbed me around my waist and tossed me onto the river like a sack of potatoes. I would've yelled at him, except he'd stretched me out in chest deep water now, and if he let go of me, I was dropping like a block of cement. So I obeyed. I moved my arms just like I'd seen him do.

"Good, now just twist your head like you are turning it in and out of the water, but don't put it in the water yet."

I did so, my chin dipping into the Suwannee.

"Add your legs now. Kick."

I kicked up a ruckus. Zippy was on shore barking like crazy. I think he was worried I was drowning. He was not alone in that.

Right then, Hank dropped his arm away from under me. I moved forward about two inches and knew I was a goner. I was just about to shriek his name, when his arm was back under my belly.

"You were swimming!" he yelled.

"I was drowning. Don't do that again."

"I'm going to push you towards shore. Keep stroking with your arms and kicking. If you feel yourself going under, just stand up."

"No…."

Too late, he propelled me towards Lightning who stood with Zippy watching their waterlogged mistress from shore. I shut my mouth and did a modified doggy paddle. Somehow, I made it the ten feet to shallow water.

Hank was a good teacher. He didn't even laugh, and I had no doubt I looked ridiculous.

"That was very good for your first time!"

I was about to object, but then we both heard the explosion of air out a blow hole, and Flash was suddenly swirling nearby. Lightning whinnied a greeting, and Zippy barked. I froze. He was very close and despite my desire to reach out and touch him, the reality of being in the water next to a six or seven-foot long creature with so many teeth was unnerving.

Hank wasn't scared at all. He flopped over onto his side and slid through the water towards Flash. This time, he didn't reach for the dorsal fin, but swam alone into the deeper water. Flash turned and swam with him, his face skimming along the surface with an eye on

Hank. Hank disappeared under the water, and so did Flash. They resurfaced almost simultaneously, now coming towards me again. It was like ballet.

Then, just as unexpectedly as Flash had appeared, he disappeared. His tail slapped down on the water and he was gone. Hank shook the water out of his hair as he stood up next to me.

"Wow." I shook my head in wonder. "Are all dolphins like that?"

"No," Hank said. "He's the only dolphin I have ever swum with. I see dolphin all the time, but Flash is the first one that ever tried to strike up a friendship. You have to be careful, though. Dolphins are really sensitive around their blowhole. You can even hurt them if you touch them too roughly and hit that."

"I won't try to touch him," I said. "Honestly, he scares me a little."

"He won't hurt you," Hank said. "But it is good to remember he is a wild animal. He won't show himself to my dad…or my friends. None of them believe me. He trusts you."

I felt honored. Liked by a big fish.

"Want to try swimming some more?" he asked.

"No. I think I have swallowed enough water for today."

Honestly, I was feeling a little sick. Swamp water on an empty stomach doesn't sit well.

Hank laughed, and walked back to shore. I followed, glancing back to see if Flash would return. He didn't. That brief visit was all we were gonna get. As Hank pulled his shirt back on, he told me, "I'll stop by tomorrow if I find out about the trailer owner. I bet you anything Kumsquat Oasis owns it though."

"Thanks." I should probably have asked him if he wanted to stay for dinner. Who could turn down canned ravioli and beef jerky strips? The problem is I only had one plate…the pan I cooked in. Tomorrow, I would buy some new canned dinners and another plate.

Hank bent down and pet Zippy, then stroked Lightning's neck.

"You got a nice family here," he said. I smiled, and picked Zippy up so he wouldn't follow Hank.

Hank turned, and jogged towards the road. The horse, puppy, and I watched him as he wove away among the reeds.

I fed Lightning and Zippy before making my own dinner. The sun was low in the sky as I settled on the stoop watching the water. It was very peaceful.

Chapter Ten

Somehow, I suffered through the next work day without managing to say anything too fire-worthy to the customers. There was one small slip of the tongue when a lady asked me if Better-Mart carried small bombs.

"Have you checked Aisle Ten?" I asked her. "It might be in the same area as our other nuclear weapons."

The lady blinked at me, and then sneered. She definitely needed to find a new dentist, but you don't need to hear the details about that.

"Young lady, you don't need to be snippy. Ant bombs!"

I had no idea what ant bombs were, and I am sure she asked for "small" bombs first, not "ant bombs". Unlike her, I was not older than the Parthenon and my hearing was stellar.

Fortunately, the cashier next to me overheard, and directed the insect-terrorist to Aisle Five.

I stopped off at the household section to buy a set of four plastic plates and bowls. Only $10.99, and now I could offer Hank dinner. I rummaged through the canned goods for something that looked like I could serve it to company. I settled upon something called "Hormel Beef Tamales." Again, they were as alien to me as Lobster Newburg, but they looked very fancy. For someone who had spent the past week ingesting Chef Boyardee Ravioli, that is not a super hard feat. I decided to grab a bag of salad, which was a splurge, but it had dressing and everything I needed in the bag.

Then I pedaled home, excitement mounting with each spin of my creaky chain. (I better look into a new bicycle chain soon.) If Hank could solve my energy problems, I could live there forever.

As soon as I pulled into my cozy cottage lot, Hank was already there. He had sprung Zippy out of his prison, and the two of them were running across the yard, in and out of the shallow part of the river, and spackling themselves with swamp goo. Lightning watched them, but didn't join in.

Glancing out at the river, I thought I caught sight of the tip of a dorsal fin, but it disappeared. It wouldn't surprise me if Flash would show up around now. He always seemed to appear when we were in some sort of super happy or super desperate state.

Hank waved as I got off my clunking bike. In no time, Zippy was wiping all the swamp goo all over my single pair of work pants. I made a note to myself that a second pair of pants was not a bad idea, now that I was rolling in dough. Besides, they were only $5.99 at Better-Mart.

"Be right back," I called, and shoving Zippy aside, dashed out of his reach and into the trailer. I threw my groceries on the counter and hurried to the back bedroom to change out of my swamped pants. I emerged in a few seconds, wearing my play clothes. Plopping on the ground so Zippy could tug on my shorts and lick me a proper hello, I steeled myself for whatever Hank had discovered. Maybe it's some sort of mind-reading talent, but I could tell he knew something and was busting to tell me.

"I found out who owns the place," Hank said, dropping down beside me, "And you will never believe it."

I waited, pondering anyone I would not believe owning this dump. Pretty much *everyone.*

"I give up. Who owns it?"

"My dad."

"Your *dad*? And you didn't know that?"

"He *didn't* until yesterday. The guy who lived here left about twenty years ago. Dad knew the guy, said he used to work at Dolphin World and wanted to be on the water. When Dad would come out to the fishing cottage, sometimes he'd run into the guy. He was a strange dude, a loner. And didn't have much money. So Dad would bring him groceries now and then. Paid his utilities a couple times. This was all before I was born, and Dad never mentioned this to me. Anyway, he lost his job, and deserted the trailer. After the dude left, Dad assumed he'd gone bankrupt and sold the land. It turns out, he owned it all the way till his death."

I blinked, not following at all. How did the land end up belonging to Hank's father?

"So it turns out he died just a month ago. Lived by himself in a nursing home near Jacksonville. He left a will and guess who he deeded the property to?"

"Your dad?"

"Isn't that wild!? Maybe Dad was the only one that was ever nice to him. Dad just got a call yesterday when I walked in the door, right after seeing you and telling you I would try to find the owner. The lawyer handling the will needs Dad to come and sign some stuff, and this piece of heaven is his."

While this story was what you call an *amazing coincidence,* I didn't see any cause for smiling. I doubted Hank's dad would go along with a plot to let an underage high school dropout continue to squat on his property.

"So I told him about you."

Here I startled, and almost grabbed Hank by the throat.

"Now don't get all worried. I told him I had a friend working full time before starting college who needed a cheap place to stay. I asked if I could get the place fixed up to pass code, could we rent it to you?"

"Starting college?"

"You'll need your GED first."

"What's that?"

"It proves you can test at a high school graduate level."

"What makes you think I can...or that I want to go to college?"

"It doesn't matter. I just didn't want to lie about your age, or get him all suspicious. You *are* working full time, and it *is* before starting college."

"But I'm *never* starting college."

"Never say never. I'm hoping to start college but I need more money than I have. Might be a while. I want to study marine biology. Flash sparked that interest. Anyway, the point is he said yes. You'll need to vacate for a couple of days so he can come and look at the place. He'll want to see it before he commits for sure, but I don't want him asking questions about your stuff all over the place."

"Where will I go? Where will Lightning go?"

"You can stay in the fishing cottage. I already told him I offered to let you stay there a couple of days. There isn't much I need to do on the trailer. Get screens. Check the wiring…the plumbing. It's old and rusty, but it looks sound enough…surprisingly. Might have to dump the couch and get you real furniture. A real bed. Regardless, I just don't want Dad to know you have already been living here."

"I can't leave Lightning," I said. I meant it too, though the thought of a real bed and real furniture, electricity and water was mighty tempting. I would've thrown Granny under the bus for that (as would you, if you knew my Granny), but not Lightning.

Hank squinted at my horse, standing nearby munching reeds.

"I'll find a friend to keep her. It's just a short time. I can get the windows fixed right away, and with Dad's connections, we can get an inspector in tomorrow. We just have to pray there's nothing really wrong with the place. I bet we could move the furniture out of the fishing cottage and into this place since Dad's selling that anyway."

I scrutinized his face. What was he after? I know what most of the boys I met were after…but it didn't seem like Hank was that sort. For one thing, Flash liked him, and I got the sense that Flash was picky and a good judge of character.

"What?" Hank asked. He must've noticed I was looking him over like he was a couch with evidence of bedbugs. (Unlike Lobster Newburg, I had PLENTY of experience with couches with bedbugs.)

"I just don't get what is in it for you," I said finally.

Hank shrugged.

"I'm not gonna sleep with you," I added, pretty bluntly I will admit, but might as well get those cards on the table.

Hank chuckled. "Thanks for the warning. That's called statutory rape. I'm not into that sort of thing."

"So what are you after?"

"Nothing. You looked like someone that needed a little kindness. Like what you showed to Lightning. And to Zippy. It was…inspiring."

Me? Inspiring? A lot of adjectives had been tossed my way over the years and not once had that word been among them. It kind of made me want to cry.

"So you'll do it?" he asked. He looked hopeful, his head tilted, eyebrows raised.

"If you can find a place for Lightning."

"You know, there's a big oak at the end of the pier out to the house. I bet we could tie her there. You can't see it from the road."

"I never tie her," I said.

"It will only be a day or two."

"I'll be at work. I hate to leave her tied all day."

"I'll check on her. Com'on Leah. This will work. And I didn't even tell you the best part."

"There's more? He left an inheritance for the new renter?"

"Well, in a manner of speaking. He was a dolphin trainer."

"Wow. But you said he lost his job…he must not have been a very good one."

"Or maybe too good. I did a little snooping and found out why he lost his job. He kidnapped the dolphin he was working with and released it into the Suwannee."

Now my eyes popped open. That was unexpected!

"How on earth does someone kidnap a dolphin?"

"You should read the article I found. It was pretty amazing."

"Did he get arrested?"

"Yeah, spent some time in jail too. Not long after that, the Suwannee flooded, so I guess he never bothered coming back here after his time in jail. I don't know what kind of work he did after jail, but he still owned the land here."

"But how did he get the dolphin?"

"He worked at a place called Dolphin World. It was a swim-with-dolphins joint just a few miles down the Suwannee, near the Gulf. Out of business now. He was a trainer. Guess what the dolphin's name was that he released into the Suwannee?"

I didn't have to guess. He wasn't the only person to figure out that the dolphin fit his name perfectly.

At that moment, the dorsal fin of Flash broke the surface, as if on cue.

"Dolphins live more than twenty years?" I asked.

"Apparently this one did."

I swear to God...or whoever...that's really what Hank told me happened. When I found a library in this stinking little town, I'd check it out. If you have a library near you, go ahead and look for yourself.

Chapter Eleven

Remembering my manners, I asked Hank if he'd stay for dinner. He looked concerned, and took a quick gander at Zippy's dog bowl.

"I'm eating fancy tonight," I said. "Fresh salad and tamales. Whatever those are."

Hank grinned, and asked, "Hormel?"

"Yes!"

"I'm in. My favorite."

I told him to have a seat on my front verandah, and pointed to the rusty stoop. "It won't take long."

First I grabbed a bunch of hay and tossed it out the door for Lightning. Then I filled Zippy's new bowl with water and dog chow. Once I saw my animal friends happily munching away, I dove into the trailer and began 'cooking'. Honestly, this was the first time I had ever made dinner for anyone. I was not up on the finer points of home entertaining. Lack of food has a way of putting the kibosh on being the hostess with the most-est. So I was a little nervous. I dumped some salad in two new bowls, and sprinkled a little of the dressing packet over them.

Then I fired up my Coleman, put it on the lowest heat setting, and carefully arranged the tamales in the bottom of the pan. With a deep sigh of come-what-may, I headed out the door with the salads in hand.

Hank took his, and pointed out to the river. There was Flash, hunting for his own dinner I suspect. His fin and sleek back curved out of the water and then submerged every few seconds.

"Oh! Forks!" I said.

I darted back in the kitchen and ripped open my new package of cutlery. They had pretty bright red handles. Fanciest forks I'd ever seen.

I handed a fork to Hank, and then plopped down beside him.

"Those tamales will just be a minute. This is our first course."

I was about to dig in, but Hank was looking at me, like he expected something.

"What?" I asked.

"Would you like me to say Grace?"

I blinked.

"Why?"

"To thank God for the meal."

I didn't know what Grace was, other than my last name. Frankly, I had seen very little grace in my life, and it was hard to be thankful for peanut butter every day for sixteen years so I hadn't had much practice in gratitude at mealtimes.

"What did God do?" I asked. "I bought the salad, the stove, *and* the tamales. Are you one of those religious fanatics?"

Hank smiled. "I can just thank Him silently."

"No, it's fine. Go ahead and thank Him for both of us. If He's listening, He might notice a few other things around here that need His attention."

"He might," Hank agreed. Then he bowed his head and closed his eyes. I kept mine open, because Zippy was getting dangerously close to my salad. I didn't think dogs were vegetarians, but he seemed mighty interested and this was the first green food I had had in months.

"Dear Lord, I thank you for this beautiful day and for the good news about the trailer. Thank you for your provision and this delicious meal Leah has so kindly offered. Amen."

Again, I took exception to that bit about *His* provision, but kept it to myself. We dug into the salad, and watched Flash in the distance, his fin appearing and disappearing in the glassy water.

I finished my salad in one tenth of the time it took Hank to eat. When you are used to fighting for your food, you learn to gobble. Besides, I was worried about burning my tamales.

They were fine. I flipped them over with one of my new forks, and dished them out onto the two new plates. I know for most people, this would not be newsworthy, but to have real hot food, on brand new plates, and eating them with forks with shiny red handles was about the most civilized thing I'd ever done.

Hank took his plate from me, and told me I had done a great job with the tamales. I agreed. No sense arguing over such an obvious fact. They were warm, not burned at all, and delicious!

"Hormel makes great beef stew also," Hank said, in between bites.

I nodded, adding it to my mental shopping list.

"When do I need to leave?" I asked.

"I don't think Dad will drop by until the inspector comes. He's got a full schedule the next couple of days. Still, just to be safe, we should move your things over tonight. Hoping I can get the inspector by Wednesday. You don't have too much, right?"

"It will all fit in my backpack," I said. "All I have is the stove, the dog bowls, a few cans…oh my new dishes and cups. The rope."

I paused trying to remember if I was forgetting anything.

"Oh yeah, my work clothes. And the hay bale."

Hank chuckled. I don't know what was so funny.

"Sounds like everything you could need or want," he said.

We finished our tamales in silence. I liked that about Hank. He didn't seem to mind the fact that I wasn't very talkative. If I'd grown up with people worth talking to, I might have turned out chattier.

He helped me 'wash' the dishes with my jug of water. I added dish soap to my mental list. All the kitchen stuff fit in my backpack. Hank went to check if we'd missed anything in the bedroom. I did store my few clothes in that closet. He gathered those and rolled them in a bundle.

Then, he noticed the coil of rope on the ground by my couch. Leaning over to gather it up, he saw the edge of the Bible poking out from under the couch. I'd forgotten about the Bible. I had read a little that first night I found it, but since then, things had gotten so busy, it must've slipped under the couch and out of my mind.

Hank picked it up, and flopped it open.

"You been reading this?" he asked.

"No. I forgot I even found it," I said.

He closed it carefully, and placed it on top of the pile of clothes. Coiling the rope around his arm, he gathered the clothes and Bible.

"If you can wear the backpack, I can carry these, and the hay bale, and roll your bike over. Lightning will follow, right?"

"Probably," I said.

With a bit of sadness, I closed the door behind us. I snapped the leash on Zippy's new collar. He wasn't exactly easy to walk. He kept snagging his body on my ankles. Hank had the harder job though. He balanced the hay bale on the bike handlebars, and put the rest of the bundle of stuff under his arm. Somehow, we managed to get to the end of the pier safely. Hank used the rope to tie Lightning to the big oak. He plopped a bit of hay down, to keep Lightning entertained and we started up the pier.

If I thought I loved that little cottage from a distance, it was nothing to what I felt when Hank unlocked the door and let me in. It was the most beautiful little house I had ever been in. It goes without saying that my experience with luxury of any sort was about as big as a turnip.

"What about Zippy?" I asked. "When I'm at work, what do I do with him? He thinks the world is his toilet."

"We can lock him in the bathroom. I'll put paper down on the floor."

Hank helped me unload my kitchen supplies, and then pointed at the refrigerator.

"There's plenty of stuff in there. Have whatever you want."

He pulled it open. It was chock full. I can't even begin to tell you all that was in there.

"I keep it stocked for when I was working in here. I'm just about finished now. So you'd do me a favor if you finish all that food."

Well, if he put it like that, who was I not to help out? I grabbed a peach from the bottom shelf. Man, I hadn't had a peach in about ten years! Juice dribbled down my chin but I didn't even have time to swipe it away before I'd made history of that peach.

"Yum," I said.

"Let me show you around. It's pretty small, but here's the bathroom."

He opened a door. I stepped inside. "Running water?"

He laughed, and flicked the faucet on. Water poured out. I musta died and gone to heaven!

Then he led me down the hall.

"This is the bedroom. Nothing fancy, but the sheets are clean."

I peeked in. Sheets. I hadn't slept under sheets in at least as long a time as I hadn't had a peach. I had a grungy thin blanket back in home sweet home with the folks. My 'pillow' was a rolled up coat, which doubled as my coat in the winter.

Maybe in Hank's eyes, this was nothing fancy, but sheets and a real pillow were the stuff of dreams in my world.

"After the inspection, we'll move all this stuff to your trailer. We already have a buyer interested in this place."

I sighed. I knew of course I couldn't stay in the cottage, but it made me sad anyway.

"Do you need anything else for now?" he asked.

"I don't need anything else *ever*!"

He carefully placed the Bible on the little end table by the bed. "You have electricity. You can read this now if you want when you lie down at night."

I picked up the Bible. "Do you read this?"

"Every day."

"Why?" I wasn't being a smart aleck. I really was curious. He looked normal enough, though nicer for sure than most people I knew. Still. He didn't look like the type to get all holy-roller on me.

"I think it's true."

"What do you mean true? It's a bunch of things we shouldn't do, right?"

"Some. Mostly it's about who God is and why we should trust Him."

"Why should we?" I could see why someone who had a refrigerator full of peaches might be inclined to trust the goodness of God, but trust me when I say I didn't have quite the same outlook.

"Find out for yourself."

"Where do I start?"

"The beginning isn't a bad place," Hank said. "You told me you like to read. The bible is a great piece of literature, if nothing else."

I tossed it onto the bed. "OK. I'll try to work it into my busy schedule."

I followed Hank back outside, and we leaned against the railing on the little dock.

"Does it make you sad to sell this place?" I asked.

"It does a little. Unfortunately, we have to. Mom was just diagnosed with MS. Her doctor bills are adding up, and all the things we have had to do on the house to make it safe for her. I was the only one that ever used the hut anyway."

"What's MS?" I asked. The refrigerator full of peaches didn't seem quite as wonderful anymore. I suspected MS wasn't a good thing.

"Multiple Sclerosis. It's a disease that attacks the nerves. She's losing balance a lot, muscle control. It's nasty."

"That stinks."

"Yeah." He sighed and pushed away from the rail. "And I better be heading out. They don't know where I am and probably could use my help."

He started down the pier. "See ya tomorrow. I'll stop by and bring a tub of water out for Lightning, and some hay. I'll check on Zippy too and take him for a walk."

I watched his back.

"Thank you," I called.

He waved without turning. I think the talk about his mom had depressed him. Talk about my mom depresses me too, but for totally different reasons.

I visited Lightning one last time before heading to bed. There was a small pond not far from the Kumsquat Oasis, and I rode her there to get a good, long drink of water. She seemed grateful. She started back on her own towards my trailer, but I steered her back to the pier and the oak tree.

"Sorry girl, but this is our home for a couple of days."

She didn't act upset as I tied her to the tree. I left a good length of rope so she could nibble the surrounding grass and reeds, and lie down if she wanted to.

By the time I returned to the hut, the sun was setting. The water was very still. I heard some loons, and osprey but it was mostly quiet. The water reflected the last rays of sun so brightly that they seared into my eyeballs. When I closed my eyes, a neon stretch of blinding white blazed across my sight.

I stuffed the whining little dog in the bathroom, and then remembered we hadn't put papers on the floor. Where would Hank have stashed papers? Rummaging through the cabinets in the kitchen, I found one full of fishing magazines. I hoped those were the papers he meant. Zippy kept snatching one or two from the pile beside me, but eventually I covered the floor with open magazines. After filling his water bowl, and putting it under the sink, I made him a little bed with a towel. This was a luxury he better not get used to. I added towel to my mental shopping list.

He curled up on the towel right away. I guess he was tired out from our busy move. As soon as I closed the bathroom door, he started whimpering but I stayed tough. I knew he would make a mess of this gorgeous hut if I left him loose all night.

The first thing I did when I went in the bedroom was open the window. The water, being right beneath the dock, lapped at the reeds with a soft rhythmic watery song. It was very comforting. By now it was dark in the house. I had forgotten all about electric lights, since I had been without them for such a long time. I flopped onto the bed, listening to the water for a long time.

Then I remembered what Hank had told me. The Bible lay next to me on the soft bed. I can't remember ever being so comfortable. Flicking on a little lamp that was perched on the end table, I opened the Bible to page one.

The Beginning

1 In the beginning God created the heavens and the earth. 2 Now the earth was formless and empty, darkness was over the surface of the deep, and the Spirit of God was hovering over the waters.

3 And God said, "Let there be light," and there was light. 4 God saw that the light was good, and he separated the light from the darkness. 5 God called the light "day," and the darkness he called "night." And there was evening, and there was morning—the first day.

6 And God said, "Let there be a vault between the waters to separate water from water." 7 So God made the vault and separated the water under the vault from the water above it. And it was so. 8 God called the vault "sky." And there was evening, and there was morning—the second day.

9 And God said, "Let the water under the sky be gathered to one place, and let dry ground appear." And it was so. 10 God called the dry ground "land," and the gathered waters he called "seas." And God saw that it was good.

The next morning, when I awoke, I realized I never got any further than that, but had fallen asleep with the words, *it was good* repeating like an echo in my head. I had slept so soundly that I had to skedaddle to get myself up and out and my friends fed and cared for before dashing off to work.

But as I pedaled top speed across the dusty road, my mind was singing in cadence to the clunk of the chain, *it was good, it was good, it was good.*

Chapter Twelve

"Young lady! Are you listening to me?"

I wasn't but I could definitely NOT admit that to the old bat who was clearly ticked off at me about something.

"I asked you three times if you could direct me to the aisle with Noxema Beauty Cream."

I will be the first to tell you that she had clearly had trouble finding that particular product for some time. Either that or Noxema should be fined for false advertising.

These are the sorts of things that are always on the verge of flowing out of my mouth. I don't know how I manage to keep them under wraps.

"I'm sorry," I said, ripping my thoughts back from the mindless task of stocking the shelf with can after can of dog food. "Beauty products are on Aisle 7." I pointed in the general direction of Aisle 7.

She didn't even say thank you. Beauty may be only skin-deep, but the lack of beauty sure isn't. At least not in her case.

I had been daydreaming about a computer. Now that I was going to have electricity, I could power the computer. The more I thought about how desperately I wanted to never work another hour at Better-Mart, the more I wanted to get started on my book. My next paycheck, I could get the computer…except, maybe not if I was going to be paying rent. Life is way too expensive. This little aside is in case you haven't noticed that disturbing truth.

I had a brief lapse of plotting how I could steal a computer, but it didn't last long. My parents had been great role models in what NOT to do. I didn't want to end up like them. Drugs, alcohol, and a life of petty theft worked for them, but definitely ruined my childhood.

So instead, I would have to save up for the computer a little at a time, and tough it out at Better-Mart for however long it took. I clawed my way through each painful moment, and finally my shift was over. With more than a little relief, I raced out the door, almost taking out an old man with a cane on my rush to freedom. Fortunately, he was a forgiving sort, and after I retrieved his bag of Better-Mart goodies, he even thanked me for brightening his day with my smile.

I admit I felt like a heel after that and slowed down. It was blistering hot. June in Florida is not the stuff of dreams. I heard July and August were even less so. Fortunately, it was cooler right on the banks of the Suwannee.

Lightning nickered when she saw me. A huge plastic tub filled to the brim with water was beside her. I couldn't for the life of me imagine how many trips back and forth from the hut poor Hank had to make to fill that!

I visited with her briefly, and promised to be back as soon as I changed my clothes and snatched Zippy out of his prison. You probably don't want to hear about what I found when I opened the bathroom door. I will spare you the details, but it took a lot of breath holding to get that place even *close* to back to breathable.

I leashed the little dog, wondering how one small creature could cause such havoc, and we hurried out the door to the eager Lightning. Untying her from the tree, she plodded along behind us as we hurried over to my plot of land. I saw a strange truck parked next to the trailer and considered turning around but then Hank appeared around the corner, his arms loaded with the old ripped screens.

"Hey Leah!" He waved, dropping the mess into a pile that included the couch, and some rusty pipes.

"Wait till you see the place!" he said.

"Whose truck?" I asked.

"That's Dad's. He let me borrow it to haul the old screens and couch away. I switched out some rusted pipes under your sinks, and cleaned things up a bit, put in new screens. The inspector shows up later this afternoon. Dad called in some favors."

I unhooked Zippy's leash, and the dog and horse both trotted immediately to the water. They both stood knee deep in the cool river while Hank led the way into the trailer.

I could not believe my eyes. Hank had done a lot more than replace screens and pipes. All the dusty, moldy looking linoleum in the kitchen had been ripped up and replaced with a clean simple pattern of faux tile. The kitchen was very small, but still, that was a feat. It seemed like way more than a day's worth of work. The window sills looked freshly scrubbed. The old skanky fixtures in the bathroom had been replaced with gleaming new ones. The bedroom had new screens, with the windows sparkling clean, and get this – bright new yellow curtains! All the windows had new blinds in them.

"Do you like it?" he asked.

"How did you do this in one day?" I really could not believe it.

"I had help. Dad was here part of the day, and he brought in a friend to do the floor in the kitchen. He'll be back soon. He wanted to meet you."

I looked around and felt like crying. Hank noticed.

"What's wrong? We can switch out the yellow curtains if you don't like them."

"No...they are fine. Beautiful even. Hank...I can't afford this. I don't even know what the rent might be, but..."

"We will stay in your budget. This was property Dad never expected to own. All he cares about is being able to cover the taxes. Your rent will be based on your income. That was his idea, by the way. Not mine."

I couldn't imagine a father that kind. No wonder Hank was the way he was.

"What about utilities?"

"Your water and electricity will not be any more than the fishing hut was. About $100 a month. That's without A/C...but we did some things that will keep it cooler. I caulked around the windows, put new blinds in the living room windows...keep those closed during the day. We insulated the water heater. We'll bring in just a small energy efficient refrigerator. We can put a window A/C unit in the bedroom, and just keep that one room cool."

He looked at me hopefully. That was doable. I was pulling in $1200 clear from Better-Mart.

"And rent?"

"$400."

"A month?"

He smiled at me. "Yes, a month."

I could do this. And get my computer.

"Sold."

"There is the problem of your age."

"I'm almost seventeen."

"You have to be eighteen in Florida to sign a rental agreement. I can sign the rental agreement, and you can pay me, but I can't lie to my Dad if he asks how old you are."

I looked down, dropping my head to my chest with a thud. So much for doable.

"You tell him the truth. Tell him about your parents. Show him what you've done all on your own. I think he will agree you are better off here with us helping you than back with your folks. Then, you pursue legal emancipation."

"What's that?"

"You go to court, demonstrate you can take care of and support yourself, and then follow the process. If you are legally emancipated, you are then treated as an 18-year-old, and can legally rent. You still can't drink or vote…"

I pondered this news. Drinking and voting were not on my to-do list anyway, so that didn't disturb me.

"How do you know this?"

"I researched it."

"Could the court decide not to grant me emancipation?"

"Yes…but given your history and what you've done to take care of yourself since then, I think you have a good chance."

"Could they decide to send me back to my parents?"

Hank paused here. I could guess the answer by his hesitancy.

"Then forget it," I said. Though what would I do now? Where else was I going to find an abandoned trailer where a horse, a dog, and an occasional dolphin could live?

"Look Leah, you have no choice. You told me your parents were glad to get rid of you. The court can also send a form to them where they release their guardianship of you and that is the easiest route."

I felt a glimmer of hope. I could not imagine they wanted me back. Though if they noticed the stash of money I'd taken, they might want *that* back. On the other hand, it's possible they were too drunk or stoned to notice they had ever had it.

"In the meantime, there is nothing on the rental form that asks age. I already told Dad I would rent, and then sublet the place to you. I told him it would build my work resume if I could add landlord. Honestly, I offered that so it protects him. I bring in enough to cover the rent and he knows I'm good for it. We avoid the issue of your age for now. But I think you have to pursue emancipation one way or another."

"We won't tell him how old I am? You promise?"

"I won't lie," Hank said, "But if he doesn't ask me, I won't tell him."

"What if I lie?" I asked.

"God would not approve."

"How do you know?"

"It's one of the Ten Commandments. Thou shalt not bear false witness."

"Is there a commandment *thou shalt not starve?* Or be beaten to a bloody pulp by your drunk father? If not, I don't think God has covered all His bases."

Hank didn't argue with me. I suspect that meant there were no commandments that dealt with those particular instances.

Our spiritual discussion was cut short by another truck pulling into my little swamp lot. The side of the truck said, "Florida Rental Inspection." A tall, skinny man with skin that looked like it had been ripped off a rhinoceros climbed out of the truck. Lots of older folk in Florida had similar sun-ripened skin.

Hank introduced himself and led the inspector into the house. I went to soak my ankles in the cool Suwannee. Meanwhile, I stroked Lightning's neck and thought about this emancipation business. Couldn't I just hide out for a year? My seventeenth birthday was in a month. One lousy year was all I needed. I was inclined to do that, just act eighteen and hope to escape notice.

The inspector must have finished all he needed to do inside, because now he was crawling under the trailer. I hoped he had good medical insurance. Soon he emerged, chatted some more with Hank, and then drove away, apparently unbitten by water moccasins or alligators.

"We passed," Hank said, waving a paper in the air. "Calling the utility companies now!"

He was on the phone for a few minutes, walked to his truck and chattered away while reading from the inspection form. I saw him pull out his wallet. I guess he was giving them credit card numbers. Which reminded me. I needed a credit card. Oh. Could a sixteen-year-old even get a credit card? Probably not. How about an emancipated sixteen-year-old? I'd have to research that.

Hank was grinning like a crocodile when he finished on the phone.

"Utilities and water hooked up tomorrow. You can move in tomorrow night."

"You're sure about the rent?" I asked.

"I promise you, Leah. If you have trouble with the rent, we will make it work."

"And you are sure your dad will rent to me?"

"Unless you make him hate you when he meets you."

"I bet I could." I wasn't bragging, either. I had a pretty good track record in that department.

Zippy must've been drinking too much Suwannee water because he began vomiting huge amounts of it, mixed in with chunks of kibble. I grabbed him when he started to re-ingest the mess.

That's when Hank's dad showed up. When I grabbed Zippy, I must have squished his upset tummy 'cause it caused him to spew a whole new quart of muck all over me.

Hank's father was already upon us, reaching out his hand. Then he saw what covered my hands, and my shirt, and he dropped it quickly.

"I'm Dan Forrest…Hank's dad," he said.

"Hi," I said weakly, "I'm Leah and this is my dog, Zippy. Sorry. He overdid it on the swamp drinking."

Mr. Forrest looked at the horse and at Hank with a raised eyebrow. I would bet the rent Hank hadn't mentioned Lightning.

"Is this your horse?" he asked.

I remembered what Hank had said about not bearing false witness. Now, *I* considered Lightning to be mine, but technically, she probably wasn't. Something inside me clenched tight when I almost said yes.

"She adopted me," I said instead.

He nodded, and didn't press me for any more information. Covered in dog puke and a horse thief. I suspected the rental agreement was being shredded inside his head.

"Hank tells me you are working full time?"

"Yes sir. I work at the Better-Mart. Been there three weeks now."

"You like it?"

Thou shalt not bear false witness. Dang, where was this new voice coming from?

"Well, my real goal is to be a writer. But I need to pay the bills."

That sounded very grown up.

"Where you from?"

"Up north. Born in Pennsylvania."

"What brought you to Florida?"

This I had not been prepared for.

"I was thinking about going to school for marine biology," I said, remembering the discussion with Hank. It was not strictly a lie since I was thinking about it…just not for me.

"Florida is a great place for that!" he said, "And you probably know that's Hank's dream too."

Hank lifted an eyebrow as I snuck a quick look in his direction.

"He mentioned it," I said.

"We talked about Hank signing a lease and you subletting from him. $400 a month…if it passes inspection."

"It passed," Hank said.

"Already?"

"You just missed him. He suggested we add insulation to the ceiling, just above the drop down tiles. Said it would decrease cooling bills. But it passed. Utilities turned on tomorrow."

"Wow." Mr. Forrest shook his head turning back to me. "I don't know if Hank shared the whole story with you but it's been a bit of a miracle. Totally unexpected. I guess it is fortuitous that you happened to arrive just when we needed a renter."

Now that was classy. I knew perfectly well they didn't *need* a renter. I imagine they could have sold the land, and made way more than they were going to make renting to me. How kind to make me feel like I was doing them a favor.

I smiled at Mr. Forrest and told him in full sincerity, "It does feel like a miracle."

"What do you want to write about one day?" he asked.

Another question I wasn't totally prepared for. Since he was being so nice, I figured I owed him another honest answer.

"I don't really know. I thought maybe I would write a novel about a kid who runs away from home and makes friends with a bunch of wild animals. Maybe a dolphin."

"Well! You have a vivid imagination."

"I'd want it to be a hopeful book. Make people laugh but make them think things could be better."

"Have you ever tried publishing your writing?"

"No, but once I won a contest in school. We had to write an essay about who we most admired and why. I even won some money, and it was published in the yearbook."

"And who did you write about?"

I smiled, remembering that essay. Bunches of kids wrote about their parents, and then there were the expected oodles of essays about Gandhi, Lincoln, and Washington. I chose a slightly different tack.

"A homeless guy who used to live under the railroad bridge in my town."

"Hmmm." Mr. Forrest cocked his head. "Why?"

"He was really old, and had been there forever. I don't remember him ever not being there my whole life. All the kids made fun of him. Some threw stones at him. I don't even know how he survived. I guess he got food somewhere, but I never saw him anywhere but under the bridge. A pond was right alongside that overpass, and sometimes I would see him fishing. Maybe he ate the fish he caught, though I never saw him catch a fish.

"Anyway, one day when I was walking by the bridge on my way to school, some of the kids from the really nice neighborhood across from ours were up ahead of me. I saw them catch a skinny old stray dog. There were a lot of strays that used to hang out near the garbage bins behind a diner right next to the bridge. Those boys took that poor skinny stray and threw him as far as they could out into the cold water. It was just meanness. The dog wasn't bothering them at all.

"The old man took off his coat and jumped in that freezing water. He swam out to the dog who looked like he didn't have the strength to paddle at all. Then he brought the dog to the underpass, wrapped him in his coat, even though he himself was shivering like a jackhammer and had to be frozen to the bone. Winters in Pennsylvania are really cold. Not like here."

"That's a sad story," Mr. Forrest said.

"It gets sadder. That was the last time I ever saw him. He wasn't there the next day...or the next. Or ever again. I guess he got pneumonia and died. I don't know what happened to the dog."

"What did the boys do?" Hank asked.

"They laughed, and then they yelled some nasty things at the old man. They threw some stones, and left."

"I imagine you wrote a mighty fine essay," Mr. Forrest said.

"I wish I kept it. I don't remember all I said, but I remember that I wanted to grow up to be more like the homeless man than those rich boys with their fancy houses."

It did occur to me that I was a lot like the homeless man...at least in respect to not having a home.

I think that might be what crossed Mr. Forrest's mind too, because he patted me on my shoulder, carefully avoiding the dog puke.

"Well, let's go sign that lease. It sounds like you will be ready to move in tomorrow."

I was so glad he never asked my age. I could not have lied to him, for sure.

Chapter Thirteen

When I got home from Better-Mart the next day, the huge tub of water had been moved from the fishing hut grounds to my own plot of land. It was right next to the mobile home, carefully placed in the shade of the live oak tree near the dog pen I'd constructed. It was filled again to the brim. I saw a brand new water hose curled around a neat holder next to the bin. The other end was hooked to a spigot on the side of the mobile home.

Zippy was in the pen, and Lightning stood nearby. I didn't see any sign of Hank, except of course, his handiwork. I went up the rusty stairs, and slowly opened the door.

It was even more wondrous than I had imagined. Lights were on, and the hum from a small refrigerator broke the usual silence. The living room had a small blue couch flanked by two end-tables. A matching recliner was on the far wall, near the window. Sun streamed in and fell on the chair. A perfect place to read and look out at the river!

All my dishes and cups were neatly stacked in the cupboards. On the counter were two unexpected surprises. A coffee maker and a toaster! The Coleman stove was on the counter too, but I wouldn't need that anymore. Just to make sure, I turned the knob on the kitchen stove to *high*. The coils on the stove top turned red. I flicked it off with a groan of delight.

The bathroom had a small yellow bath mat, a white and yellow checkered shower curtain, and a yellow towel on the rack! Hank had even bought toilet paper and soap. I peeked behind the shower curtain. A bottle of shampoo sat on a small caddy hooked to the shower head.

The small bedroom was almost filled completely with the bed from the fishing hut that I had slept so soundly on. The sheets and white comforter, and soft pillow I'd so admired were smoothed and tucked in place. One end-table with a small lamp flanked the right side of the bed with my Bible placed nearest the bed. On the wall opposite the window, a small dresser stood. I opened the closet door. My one pair of extra work pants were hung neatly beside my two t-shirts.

Zippy was barking up a storm outside, but I couldn't move. It was like I was paralyzed. I dropped onto the bed, mouth hanging open, and tears flowing like Mount Vesuvius down my face.

There was nothing more I needed in the whole wide world. I could not believe this was my home. I don't know how long I sat there, crying like a big old baby, but it was a while.

Finally, I went to the sparkling bathroom, washed my face with my sweet smelling soap, turned on the faucet and let the water run over my fingers. It was like liquid gold, that running water. I splashed it on my face, washing away all traces of the tears. Then I dried my face on the soft yellow towel. Never, not once in my life, had I felt so clean, so new, so hopeful!

I went to grab a flake of hay for Lightning, and realized the hay was gone. Well, it was the only thing missing. Hank was my hero. He had thought of practically everything. Heading out back to Zippy and Lightning, I noticed a rectangular wooden enclosure. I'd missed it at first, since it was on the far end of the house. The top had a latch. I pulled it open. There was the hay bale! Hank must have built this little hay shed.

Again, I have no idea how he did all of this in one day. Maybe he had angels helping him. It sure didn't seem humanly possible.

I lifted Zippy out of the pen, and got rewarded with another full face washing. Lightning nuzzled me briefly but then she started nibbling at the open hay bin. I pulled a flake off for her, and closed the bin.

Zippy and I headed to the water. I plopped down, not caring at all that my one set of 'play clothes' would be soaking wet.

"Zippy, I think I need a bathing suit."

Man, that water felt good! It would cool off tonight, and I would open all the windows to let the cool air in. If I closed them and shut all the blinds during the day, maybe my home would stay cool.

Lightning must have finished her hay, because she ambled over and stood in the water with us. Zippy had fun pouncing after the tiny fish that tickled my ankles.

We all startled when we heard the whoosh of air from Flash's blowhole. He was right in front of us, not twenty feet away.

"Hi Flash!" I called.

He dipped back underwater, and I was afraid he was gone for good. Instead, he surprised me surfacing five feet closer. He skimmed the surface, lifting his face above the water.

Dolphins are supposed to be as smart as humans. I believe it. Looking into Flash's eye, I felt certain he knew exactly what a monumental day it was for me. He was here to wish me well, and celebrate with me. I knew that as certainly as I knew the earth was round and if it weren't for gravity, we'd be flying off into outer space.

Zippy barked and yipped, jumping into the water. I thought it would scare Flash off, but he was almost motionless, watching us. Then he smacked his snout up and down on the water, and let out a series of high pitched squeals. Zippy tumbled back and darted out of the water, hiding behind me. Lightning whinnied.

I tried to imitate the sound Flash made. I have a pretty good memory, and so I think I did a passable imitation of whatever Flash had said to me.

Well you would have loved the reaction I got to that! Flash submerged and then flung himself into the air in one of the most acrobatic leaps I have ever seen. He crashed back into the water so nearby that we all were sprayed by the splash.

He did that over and over again, each leap into the air more startling than the one before it. I don't know if he was showing off or rejoicing. Lightning pawed at the water, sending up her own sprays of joy. I stood up and jumped up and down, so that water was flying everywhere. I was laughing; Lightning was snorting; Zippy was barking, and Flash was leaping. What a crazy, boisterous bunch of unlikely friends!

And then there was honking, and I swung around to see Hank's car. He bounded out of the car and came running over. Dashing past us and through the water, he raised his arms above his head and dove into the river. We all stopped our clamor, breathlessly watching to see where he would reappear. His head broke the surface not far from where Flash was still leaping and crashing.

I cringed, afraid the dolphin wouldn't notice him and would come smashing down on top of him. I shouldn't have worried. Like I said, dolphins are not dumb. Flash was underwater for a few seconds and then I saw his fin pop out of the water just inches from Hank. Hank caught hold of the fin near its base and the dolphin was off to the races!

He carried Hank way up the river till I could barely see Hank's curly hair, and then circled back. He deposited Hank maybe twenty feet in front of us, chittered at me with a big smile, and disappeared.

Hank was laughing as he swam back to us.

"Wild!" he said. He crawled out of the water, and threw himself down next to me. "I think he was telling you, *welcome home.*"

"And what a welcome it was!"

"Do you like it?"

"I love it, Hank. I don't know how you did it. How did you build that hay bin?"

"That was fun!"

"And all those extras...the soap...the toilet paper..."

"I figured it had been a long time since you'd seen those."

"You were right."

"I left the blinds open so you would have the full effect. But from now on you should close those during the day. It will keep the home cooler."

"OK."

"And we will get a window AC for the bedroom. I didn't have time for it today."

"I don't see why not," I said. Then I smiled when he looked surprised.

"It feels good to be a landlord," he said.

"You would go broke if you do that for all your tenants."

"That's true. From now on you get your own toilet paper and soap."

"Deal. I have some Hormel Beef Stew. I think we have a refrigerator full of peaches to go with it. Want to stay for dinner?"

"How could I pass that up? I guess we don't have a table for you to eat on."

"That's ok. There really isn't room for one."

"No."

"I like eating outside with Lightning anyway. I hate for her to dine alone."

"I bet we could scrounge up a picnic table."

"That would be nice!"

We fell into silence, gazing out at the water, while the current sent gentle waves lapping at the shore against my back. Zippy sniffed about the underside of the mobile home. Lightning munched the tips of reeds.

The wind picked up as the sun dropped lower in the sky. Flecks of sunlight danced on the ripples and then bounced directly into my retina, blinding me. I would not have minded dying right then and there. Really. Life would probably never be better.

"That book you want to write," Hank said, "Are you writing it?"

"No. I need a computer. I figure I can get one soon. I need to save up a while first."

"I'm not sure what internet would cost here. I can check. I have an old laptop you can have. It's not fancy, but it does have a word program. You can work on your book without internet. It's yours if you want it."

Oh yea. Internet. I hadn't thought of that. But I knew he was right that I could work on the book without it and figure out how to get it to my future adoring audience later.

I turned to stare at him. He was offering me a free computer?

"Only one condition," he added.

"What's that?" I narrowed my eyes. Here it comes. I knew he was too good to be true. I was ready to grab Lightning and Zippy and walk away from all of this. I would not be used by anyone. I'd had enough abuse for a lifetime.

"You promise you really will start working on your book, and the computer is yours."

Chapter Fourteen

I promised Hank immediately. The next day, when I returned from work there was a laptop computer sitting on my couch. There was a note on it and a key.

"Remember your promise. Work on your book a little each day. Also, lock your door from now on. I installed a lock. Here is the key. You have things worth protecting now. Hank."

It was a used laptop, but in fine shape. Fortunately, I was a quick study and had learned computer use in school. We had even worked on an Acer, which is what this one was. I had gotten an A in my computer class. Computers were a bit of a refuge for me. They always behaved exactly the way you told them to. If you hit backspace, they went back a space. If you hit delete, they deleted. They were a welcome respite from my world where the parents that were supposed to be my protection against the world were instead my biggest threat. Nothing was logical in that part of my life.

Anyway, mournful thoughts *go away.* I opened the laptop, and it burst into life. I didn't have internet, obviously, so I went directly to the word documents, chose "blank page", and began my story.

It was easy to write. I hadn't had the tools or the leisure to write much while growing up in my little hovel in Hell. But I had a great memory and a long list of grievances I needed to get off my chest.

What better way to rip demons out of me than to expose their deeds like sewer rats facing daylight?

I had written 5,000 words before it registered that the puppy was chewing on my toes begging for dinner, and Lightning was nickering for her hay. Come to think of it, I was hungry myself.

Wait till you hear what I had for dinner! FRESH salad topped with ranch dressing, toasted bread with real butter on it, and Dinty Moore Stew. I still couldn't quite bring myself to pick up fresh meats, since they cost a whole lot more than canned dinners. I would work up to that.

I sat outside on my stoop, watching the sunset while eating. My friends all munched and grinded teeth nearby. I half expected Flash to show up, but he didn't. I wondered if he had any other friends he could hang out with. He had never shown up with another dolphin. Always alone. I felt bad for him. Now that I had friends, I realized how lonely I had been. Funny how if you've grown up without ever knowing something, you don't know how much you missed it…or needed it. I guess that's one advantage of a deprived childhood.

Hank didn't show up either. But I thought of him after I scrubbed my pot, and my dish. The sun had set, but with the flick of a switch, *let there be light!*

That's from the Bible. I knew that because I had started reading it. Since it meant so much to Hank, I felt like I owed him that much. Retrieving the Bible from the bedroom, I curled up on my comfy new couch and settled happily against the arm. Zippy hopped onto my lap and started nibbling on the Bible cover.

"No," I said sternly. He startled because I never reprimanded him. Not even when I saw the bathroom floor he had personally converted into an overflowing toilet.

He stopped chewing my Bible and started in on the fringed edge of my shorts. I was only up to Genesis 6, which was titled: *Wickedness in the World.* Man, could I relate to that! I was totally with God in thinking He had made one giant mistake in creating humanity. I was cheering Him on with that whole worldwide flood business. Until I considered Noah. You've probably heard the story of Noah and the Ark. Even I had, though it never occurred to me to think of it as true, the way Hank seemed to. Listen to what the Bible says about Noah:

Noah was a righteous man, blameless among the people of his time, and he walked faithfully with God.

This gave me pause. It sounds like Noah alone of all the mess of people on the earth was worth saving. I think it was on his coattails of righteousness that his wife and kids and their wives were allowed to hop on the Ark. It made me consider something I had never really thought much about. *One person can make a difference.*

See, I grew up in a world of wickedness. Nothing seemed worth preserving in the dregs of humanity that peopled my corner of the planet. However, as I considered the individuals who had been in my life, there were some that gave me hope. Miss Gribbs the librarian. Miss Beam at Better-Mart. Hank. Hank's dad. That might be all, which further cemented my belief that the vast bulk of humans were not worth the dirt they were formed from. However, reading about Noah, and how his family was saved because of him, not to mention all the animals and birds, made me ponder. One single decent man changed the world.

That's if you believe Genesis 6…or any of the Bible. I can't say as I did. Sounded mighty suspicious to me. But something doesn't have to be strictly true in order to be inspiring. I have to admit, I was inspired by Noah.

He set about building that boat all by himself. I bet all the wicked neighbors were making fun of him. I'd been the brunt of ridicule enough to know it doesn't take much to make the mob decide to pick on someone who's a little different.

I knew a little bit about geography and Noah didn't live anywhere near an ocean. This was not a boat you just go stick on a pond for a day of fishing for carp. This was a massive boat. I could figure that out even without knowing exactly how big a cubit was.

To fit two of every creature onboard, it had to be humongous. Doesn't take a genius to figure that out. So here is this one righteous man, while everyone else is evil to the core, building a gigantic boat in the middle of the desert. I suspect it took him quite a while. It doesn't sound like he had any helpers. I didn't discover in my reading exactly how long, but again, a little common sense goes a long way. Had to be months…or years of work!

All the while, the bad guys were likely pelting him with spit wads, and nasty comments. God only told *Noah* why he was building the boat. As far as I could see, no one else was privy to that info.

Noah must have felt misunderstood, picked on, bullied. He cannot have had an easy time of it. But he didn't give up. The Bible says Noah obeyed God in everything.

I decided that one chapter gave me enough to fertilize my spirit for a while. I closed the Bible, and noticed little Zippy was snoring. He really needed one more walk before bedtime, but truth be told, I was not keen on walking him in the dark with all the dangerous critters that could be lurking. I carried his slack little body to the bathroom and laid him on a nice soft towel I'd folded in a corner under the sink. Hank had provided a pile of magazines, which I ripped pages from and lined a section of the floor. I hoped Zippy would make use of them. Just in case, I picked up the pretty yellow rug and put it in the shower for safety.

Flicking off the light, I crept to my bedroom. The summer night's never got really cold, but they were cooler, and the breeze off the Suwannee was strong enough to lift the curtains when I opened the window. The full moon looked like it was sitting on one of the live oak trees across the river. It perched there like a big fat yellow owl on the tippy top of the tree.

The light reflecting on the river was bright enough to light up the still water. Even from here, I heard the tell-tale sound of Flash's blowhole expelling air as he surfaced and then saw the distinctive dorsal fin with a notch in the middle.

He must've been fishing, because he disappeared, and then I saw some splashes like fish panicking. Maybe herds of shrimp. (Herds? Packs?) This went on for at least twenty minutes. I sat in the dark, watching him. Me and the moon.

Apparently, my vigil was not the only one. Lightning nickered, and then Flash lifted his head out of the water, and answered with the *eheheheh* sound that only a dolphin can make. I tried imitating him out the open window, but it was a poor excuse for dolphin speak.

Lightning whinnied again, probably to encourage me. She was that sort of horse. She took the smallest things to encourage and magnified them. Like when I first rode her, and she responded so perfectly to my sorry state of horsemanship, acting as though I knew what I was doing. I could take some lessons from her in terms of thinking well of others, giving them the benefit of the doubt, and exuding optimism in the face of complete incompetence.

Of course, that's not what God did in the Noah story. He wiped all the scumbags off the earth. He didn't give any of those evil incompetents the benefit of the doubt. Not that they deserved it. I was with God on this particular mass homicide.

But I had to admit, lately I had been on the receiving end of mercy. Miss Beam had given me a job despite my age and lack of experience. Hank had offered me friendship even though I wasn't very nice to him at first. His dad gave me a house after I'd lied and hidden from him and everyone else. I really didn't deserve what those nice people offered me, but I was pretty glad they had overlooked that point.

Flash and Lightning continued their discussion for a few more seconds, and then Flash disappeared and didn't resurface. I left the blinds open, because the moon was so beautiful, and the breeze felt like cool silk drifting over me.

I lay in bed wondering about Noah. Did he warn the people about the flood that God was going to bring? Did God warn them? If either of them did, no one mentioned it in Genesis 6. So what did the people do as the waters slowly rose around them? Did they run and pound on Noah's ark, saying, "Let me in! We're sorry! We didn't mean to call you a crazy lunkhead!"

If they did, I sure wouldn't blame Noah for saying, "Nope. Sure hope you invested in swimming lessons." I would have, but it seemed out of Noah's character, from the little I'd already learned about him. I imagine if anyone knocked on the door of the ark, Noah would've opened it.

What about all the little babies? There had to have been some. Did God not care about *them* when He flooded the earth? It's not like babies are wicked, unless you count all the drool, and spit up, and gross diapers. Those are wicked, but not really moral failings. Doesn't seem like they should have been punished too.

There must be more to this story that I was missing. Hank was a good guy, with a good brain. Why would he believe in a monster, and frankly, the Noah story painted God as a monster in my mind. No doubt, a lot, if not *most* folks deserved to be left in the wake of the ark, but *everyone*??

The moon was rising, lifting off the treetops. As it crept slowly upward, it got smaller. Now I know in reality, the moon stays the same size. It looked huge from my perspective close to the horizon, but as its position changed, so did its appearance. It was the same moon…but looked entirely different when it sat in different places in the sky.

Maybe so does God.

I don't mean God moves around in the sky like the moon, though maybe He does. I wouldn't know having only gotten through the first six chapters of the Bible. I wasn't sure how he locomoted. But maybe, the way I saw Him in Genesis 6 was totally different from how I would see Him in Genesis 20. Same God, but in a different place.

It was just a thought, and a little bit crazy being as I knew next to nothing about God. I tucked the thoughts away, and watched the golden moon climbing upward. Finally, it disappeared beyond the viewing range of my window, and I closed my eyes. It was invisible to me now, but for some kooky reason, I felt comforted knowing it was still there, lighting all that blackness in the summer sky.

Chapter Fifteen

Hank showed up the next day after work. I'd already finished my fancy dinner of fresh green beans, sauerkraut, and hot dogs. I shared the hot dogs with Zippy who almost took off my fingers snatching that tasty morsel.

Hank arrived as I was sitting down on the stoop, watching the Suwannee drift along. He came to collect the rent. I wrote my first official check with my first official checkbook which had just arrived to my P.O. box the day before. How grown up of me!

He asked if I found my lodging to my liking. Did I ever! Sure it was a little warm, but I was hardly ever inside anyway. At night, the breeze drifting in off the Suwannee was enough to keep me from floating away on my sweat.

"We are installing a window AC unit in your bedroom tomorrow," Hank promised.

I thought of my view of the moon.

"Do we have to?" I asked.

"You'd be more comfortable sleeping. We could put it in the living room if you prefer, but you'd have to close off the bedroom and bathroom. It won't cool the whole trailer very well."

"I'd prefer that."

Hank shrugged. I appreciated his lack of nosiness. He didn't ask me why.

"Flash came last night," I said. "I was already in bed, but I heard him talking to Lightning."

"What did they say?"

"Eheheheh."

Hank laughed. "Lightning too?"

"She neighed, but it almost sounded like she was imitating him. I wonder what they have to talk about."

"I wonder too."

"Do you think that old guy, Flash's old trainer, had a horse?"

"I doubt it. I don't think he had much money."

We both took a gander at Lightning. The same thought probably pedaled through both our minds. Lightning didn't exactly look like a horse that would break anyone's bank.

"And it was twenty years ago. Dolphins live maybe that long. I just can't picture a horse living on its own for twenty years. Seems like someone would have caught her…"

We would likely never know.

"Do you think someone is looking for her?" I asked. This thought had worried me some. I had become really fond of Lightning. How could I give her up if someone came to claim her?

"I doubt it," Hank said. "I read that lots of people just sell old horses at auction, and they get bought cheap for slaughter."

"Why would someone buy them just to kill them?"

"Most go overseas for food."

"People eat horses?" I was horrified.

"The worst part isn't that they get eaten, it is how they die. They kill horses the same way they kill cattle in the slaughter house. I read about it and just about vomited. They use something called a captive bolt gun, that shoots into the brain, and then they bleed out the animal. But some people say the horse's brain is different from cattle, and the shot doesn't necessarily kill him. Some of them are just paralyzed, and actually feel the full horror of being skinned alive."

I was back to thinking about Noah and how a worldwide flood wasn't brutal enough in knocking off humankind. Fortunately, this cheery discussion was interrupted by the sudden appearance of Flash. He hadn't come to chat this time. He was doing his stupendous leaps ten feet in the air, and crashing back with impressive belly flops.

"Why does he do that?" I asked Hank.

"Some people think it's just for fun."

"It does look fun."

"Probably dolphins do that for lots of reasons. Looking for food, busting parasites off when they crash down again in the water…that's what scientists think."

Flash had finished his acrobatics and now swam towards us, his dorsal fin rising and falling as he came near. He raised his head and whistled, then blurted several fast clicks.

"He sure talks a lot."

Hank nodded. "The strange thing is, it is really unusual for dolphins to be alone. They almost always travel in groups…they're called pods. They need each other for protection, and for fishing. They can kill a shark, but they are more vulnerable when they are loners."

"Why do you think he's alone? I have never seen him with another dolphin."

"No. Neither have I."

We watched Flash move even closer to shore, and then lift his snout out of the water and call "eheheheh" to Lightning.

"From all I've read, dolphins never travel alone. The only thing I can figure out is Flash was in captivity from birth, and when he was released, he just didn't know any better."

Poor Flash. Being a fellow dysfunctional loner, I could relate.

Hank continued. "What's pretty amazing is that he's lived so long on his own. Dolphins depend on each other for protection, especially from sharks."

"Maybe that's why he hangs out here. I never see sharks. Maybe it's safer."

"Probably. I have seen baby sharks, a little closer to the ocean though. I don't think they tolerate the brackish water well."

Lightning now stepped into the water, and snorted. Zippy perked his ears, and seeing Flash surface, dashed to the waterside as well, barking up a storm. Flash moved a little closer, and smacked his nose against the water, splashing Zippy. It looked like he was doing that on purpose to taunt the puppy, but that couldn't possibly be true.

Whether it was purposeful or not, it made Zippy go nuts. He jumped in the water, which was over his head. That surprised him, he yipped one more time at Flash, who had submerged. Then he circled back to shore, shook a spray of droplets all about, and sat down waiting.

Flash didn't return. Zippy was pretty proud of himself for having scared off a creature about a hundred times bigger than he. Lightning nuzzled the pup, as if to congratulate him.

"He's got spunk, I'll say that for him," Hank said, sitting down beside me.

"Spunk is good in this world."

Hank eyed me, but didn't comment further.

We watched in silence as the sun slowly dipped lower in the sky. I liked that about Hank. Most people feel the need to fill every second with chatter, whether they have anything worth saying or not. My personal observation is nine times out of ten they have nothing worth saying, but that doesn't seem to stop them. It is about the millionth reason why I liked my circle of animal friends so much. No one spoke unless it was necessary.

But now, I had a necessary question.

"Hank, what do you think Noah did that everyone else on earth didn't do?"

Hank turned from the gorgeous sunset and blinked at me.

"Why do you ask?"

"I have been reading the Bible, and I just don't believe that only one person on the entire earth didn't tick God off. That doesn't sound like a very safe God."

"No. He's not safe," Hank agreed, "But to tell you the truth, I am more surprised there was even one good man worth saving."

"Well what was so special about Noah?"

"We don't know much, other than he obeyed God in everything."

"Then the next world-wide flood, I'm in trouble," I said.

"Don't worry. We all are. God promised no more world-wide floods though."

"Oh. I didn't read that part."

"How far are you?"

"Genesis 6."

Hank grinned. "Really blasting through it, aren't you?"

"I am trying to understand as I go along, and I have a lot of questions. It slows me down."

"I'm just teasing," Hank said, "You are reading it exactly the way it should be read."

"Do you believe it is all true?" I asked.

"I believe all of it is true that isn't supposed to be symbolic, or poetry, or parables. Those are stories Jesus told."

"You think Noah built a huge boat and all the animals just came on their own and walked in the boat?"

"Let me ask you. A year ago would you have believed a horse and a dolphin would be friends and talk to each other?"

"No, but that's really not even close to believing the story about Noah."

Hank shrugged. He displayed no interest at all in convincing me one way or the other. He did seem interested in the sunset however, and there was good reason. I don't know if Florida is unique, but compared to Pennsylvania sunsets, Florida is like the Taj Mahal of sunsets.

Even Zippy lay down on the shore near Lightning, and watched the gorgeous colors stretching across the sky. I contemplated all the loveliness for a moment, but didn't want to lose the chance to ask all my questions Noah had raised.

"So is it still true that not a single person on earth obeys God the way Noah did?"

"There are some who tried. The Bible says we all sin, and all our works are basically filthy rags to God."

"Why doesn't He break His promise and drown us then?"

"I don't know, really. I think I would. But God is perfect, so He is perfectly trustworthy too. He can't break a promise."

"But God can do anything I thought."

"He can't go against His own character."

Interesting loophole.

Hank glanced at me, and hesitated. I could tell he wanted to say something more but wasn't sure I could take it.

"What?" I asked. "Does God have something even worse than drowning waiting for us?"

"Well…yes. There is Hell."

"I know about Hell. You believe in Hell?"

Frankly, even *I* believed in Hell because I had lived in it already.

"Yes, the Bible says Hell is real. And the people who don't follow God go to Hell."

"But you said no one follows God."

"That's the problem."

"We're all going to hell?"

"We are, except God gave us a way back to Him."

"Will I read about that?"

"Yes…but not for a while. Do you want me to tell you about it?"

"No. I think I'll wait and be surprised."

This is strange, but my heart fluttered with excitement. I had thought of God for about twenty seconds my entire life prior to finding that Bible. I know here in the south, everyone goes to church and is super holy…but where I come from, that just wasn't the case. And in my home, the only mention of God was followed by a string of four letter words that I bet Noah was not in the habit of using.

I liked the idea of some big mystery that I would solve by reading the Bible. Besides, I missed reading, and even though it was a little on the unbelievable side, so far the Bible had a pretty engaging story line.

Hank slapped his palms down on his knees, and stood up.

"Thanks for the rent check. I gotta run now. Got a new property I'm starting work on now that the fishing hut is ready for sale. We start at the crack of dawn."

Oh. The fishing hut. I hoped no one would buy it, which was a pretty uncharitable thought since I couldn't hope to afford it. If I couldn't have it, I didn't really want anyone to have it. Except Hank. But that wasn't an option.

"Hey, I almost forgot. I have something for you." Hank reached in his pocket and pulled out a folded piece of paper.

"What's this?" I asked, taking it from him.

"Read it."

I opened the flyer.

Here's what it said: Fiction Writing Contest. Open to amateur and professional writers. Deadline: September 9. Entry fee: $200. Prize: $50,000 publishing contract with Montezuma Books. Submission requirement: 50,000-70,000 word original manuscript…

I looked up.

"I can't afford to throw away $200."

"I'll make you a deal. If you get your book written, I'll pay the entry fee."

"Why?"

"Flash told me he had a good feeling about you."

For a moment, I believed him, but then I saw he was grinning.

"You've never even read anything I've written. How do you know I'm any good?"

"I don't. Will you do it?"

I shook my head looking down at the flyer.

"I've never written 50,000 words."

"Did you ever ride a horse, or play with a dolphin or rescue a drowned dog before?"

"No."

He didn't argue any more, but just cocked his head looking at me. I got his point.

"Do I have to split the money with you if I win?"

"No, but I might raise your rent a little if you win."

"I did start my book, like you told me too…but it's not fiction. It's true. It's about Lightning, and Flash, and Zippy."

"No one will believe it anyway. Call it fiction."

He had a point.

"Ok," I said, nodding slowly. "I'll try. I have three months."

"That's long enough for bunnies to have three litters of baby bunnies," Hank said. "Well, I will head out now."

After Hank left, I kissed Lightning good night and grabbed Zippy. Could I write a whole book? The story was playing out right before my eyes. All I had to do was write what I was living. How hard could that be?

I curled up on the couch with Zippy in my lap, and popped open my Bible to Genesis 7. Time to see how my old friend Noah got out of his predicament. In no time, I'd dashed along to chapter 8.

The first line in Genesis 8 almost made me drop the Bible. Listen: *But God remembered Noah and all the wild animals and the livestock that were with him in the ark, and he sent a wind over the earth, and the waters receded.*

God *remembered* Noah??? The entire world had been wiped clean of all the animals, birds, and people. The only human beings that remained were Noah and his family. How could God have *forgotten* Noah? This bugged me bigtime. Did God have Alzheimer's? That was the only explanation I could come up with.

If only eight people remained on the entire earth and God lost track of them, what hope did any of us have of capturing any of His attention when there were *billions* of us? *None!* No hope at all! There was no way He could pay attention to, all of us if He struggled to remember the ONE righteous man on earth.

I was seriously bummed.

In fact, I was so turned off to this God, that all I could do was close the book. Zippy stirred in my lap. (It's astonishing how lickety-split puppies go from full throttle to unconscious.)

I closed my eyes. It is possible, even probable, I was misinterpreting this whole remembering thing. What if Hank had just paid attention to the first facts he knew about me: age sixteen, runaway, squatting illegally in decomposing trailer. He would have a whole different picture of me, wouldn't he? It certainly wasn't the whole story.

OK God. I will give you another chance.

I flipped back to Genesis 8. I had never paid attention to all the little references in the margins while I was reading. It was hard enough just trying to understand the main text. Now I looked at the dozens of cross references to other verses linked with Genesis 8:1. I flipped the Bible open to each one. There were bunches in Genesis itself. God did a lot of *remembering,* and each time, it was clear it was of things He had obviously not forgotten. Like 'eternal covenants', and people even *I* remembered – like Abraham.

'Remember', in God's terms, didn't seem to mean the opposite of forgot. I read all the references, and some were in books I had never heard of – like Ruth, and Nehemiah. They all expressed remembering as more like 'took special notice of'. This made me feel a whole lot better. It was not that God had forgotten Noah. It was that now, as poor Noah and his merry band of homeless creatures tottered about on the rocking boat, God brought them to the forefront of His mind.

If this was the case, it was worth giving Genesis 8 a shot. Warning, just so you are prepared if you decide to follow in my footsteps, it got worse before it got better. This flood was not only world-wide, but it took a long time before even the tips of any mountains managed to shove their rocky necks above the water after the rain stopped. It took ten months for the mountain tops to be visible to Noah.

I pondered this for quite some time. Ten months with no sight of land, huddling on one boat that contained all that was left of the earth's creatures. One boat that had to supply all the food as well as contain all the food *waste* that exited all those animals' bodies. (Did they pitch it overboard? I imagine they did but even so, that was a LOT of work for just eight people.)

Genesis 8 didn't clue me in about how Noah felt during this journey. I would've been freaking out. It didn't sound like Noah was going stir-crazy, though he had to have been. He did send a dove out to hunt for dry land several times. Finally, the dove did not return.

Now at first, I had another crisis, being an animal lover. Did the dove fly around and couldn't find land, so it dropped into the sea and drowned?

I don't think so, but like I said, I am no Bible scholar. (Nor any kind of scholar.) However, the Bible said that when the dove didn't return, Noah took the cover off the ark. (This added a whole new set of questions...the ark was huge...how did he get the cover off? Maybe the elephants helped.) Any way about it, it sounded like the dove's disappearance was a positive sign. I would guess it found land, and decided it was a whole lot better than sticking around the crowded, smelly ark.

Now the story continued to get stranger. God told Noah to leave the boat with the animals, and go multiply on the wonderful new earth, freshly dry cleaned.

And Noah obeyed, and immediately built an altar. Ok, so far I was with Noah. I got that he was grateful to God for safely delivering Noah and his relatives, though He did take His sweet time about it. BUT GET THIS. Noah then sacrificed animals and birds on the altar.

Let this sink in. He just spent a lot of effort and time saving those creatures from the flood. And now the first thing he does is KILL them.

I will never understand this God. Did God chastise Noah? No. He was *pleased*. Then He promised that He would never flood the earth again, even though "every inclination of the human heart is evil from childhood."

Why save them then?

Fortunately, Genesis 8 was now finished, and I could close the Bible before my head exploded.

Chapter Sixteen

I was dying to ask someone about all these crazy things I was reading in the Bible, but that would have to wait. Another day, another dollar. My own little ark of creatures greeted me hungrily in the morning. The sun was already scorching as I stepped outside.

I closed the blinds in all the rooms, as Hank had suggested. I was glad he'd be installing the window AC today. Summer was only beginning, and it was mighty warm.

I ate my breakfast on the stoop, with Lightning nearby grinding her teeth on her hay and Zippy snorting his puppy chow. My feast was Lucky Charms. If you read the ingredients of Lucky Charms, you might wonder if it has any nutritional value. Whole grain is the first ingredient but then the next forty or so are various forms of sugar. I read that 37% of Lucky Charms is sugar. My kind of breakfast!

Breakfast itself was a novelty. Back home, breakfast was a luxury we couldn't afford. On occasion, I could scrounge up a piece of stale bread but most of the time, I just hurried off to school with nothing but the love of learning in my belly.

I had never had Lucky Charms before, but with the latest paycheck, I had enough free cash to peruse the grocery aisles. Those little marshmallow shapes called to me, and I couldn't resist.

I let Zippy lap up the last molecules of milk in my bowl. Time to go bring home the bacon! Zippy whined when I put him in his pen, but Lightning immediately came over and stuck her muzzle near for him to cuddle against. He quieted down.

I hopped on my bike and pedaled across the rutted flood plain, the bike squawking and creaking the whole way. It still amazed me that Lightning never tried to follow me to work. She would follow me every single time I went walking to get water from the Kumsquat Oasis, or to go foraging for sticks, or to just walk along the river for the fun of it. I don't know how she figured out she couldn't come with me to work, but she did.

She never tried to follow Hank anywhere. This was even more surprising because Hank was the one that dropped off her hay every week. You would think that she would follow the food source. That she *didn't* was a great comfort to me. I think she liked me, and knew I was her special friend whether I fed her or not.

I was not her owner. That much was clear. She had chosen *me.* I never tied her up, except that one time when we tied her to Hank's oak tree. She stayed with me because she wanted to.

She was on my mind especially now that Hank had told me the story about the dolphin trainer. How did she meet Flash? I felt pretty certain it had something to do with the old trainer who had freed Flash from the Dolphin encounter pen.

I'd asked Lauren, my first *sort-of* friend from the Better-Mart, where the library was. It was practically right behind the Better-Mart. I planned to sprint over there during my lunch break and see if I could find anything about the old dolphin trainer from Dolphin World.

Before my lunch break, I had to endure the crème-de-la-crème of Better-Mart customers. This one came to my register with a bag filled with clothes.

"I'd like to return these."

I pawed through the bag. The clothes were all tattered, and dirty, clearly having been worn for months, if not years.

"They're not working out," the customer added.

"Did you decide that in the past decade?" I asked.

"No need to get smart-mouthed."

"You need to talk with customer service for Returns."

"This isn't a Return. I just would like to exchange them for the next size up."

She was not the only one who would like to make an exchange. I called the Customer Service manager. Sometimes I wondered if there was reverse evolution going on.

You probably figured out that my lunch break could not arrive soon enough. I scurried out, and raced to the library. It was literally just across a scrubby field through the line of trees behind Better-Mart.

I didn't know the trainer's name, but Hank had told me the dolphin he freed was named Flash. I asked the librarian to help me, since I figured she would find what I wanted a whole lot quicker than I would.

"I am looking for news articles about Dolphin World, and a dolphin named Flash that was freed about twenty years ago."

"I remember that story!" the librarian said. "The trainer's name was Matthew Parks. I only know that because my folks didn't live too far from him, along the Suwannee."

What were the odds???

"Did you know him? Did you see where he lived?"

"He kept to himself. I know he traveled down the Suwannee by boat to work at that dolphin petting place. A strange man. Real loner. My parents saw him now and then at the local grocery store. But he was antisocial. Never talked to anyone. However, he loved his animals."

"Animals?"

"Honestly we were all rooting for him when we heard about how he freed that dolphin. Nowadays, you hear more and more of an uproar about how dolphins and killer whales shouldn't be in the small pens they live in for the dolphin shows…but back then, you heard almost nothing. Still, Dolphin World was about as bad a place like that as I'd ever seen. The poor dolphins lived in shallow small pools of water. I was just a little kid but even I knew it was a dirty, sad, unhealthy place for them. But in the end, Matthew Parks was fined and arrested. The good news was Dolphin World went out of business not long afterwards."

"Did he have other animals?"

"We never saw his property up close. He didn't like people coming near, but we heard dogs often enough when we passed by on the road.

"Did he have a horse?"

She looked at me strangely, and shook her head.

"Not that I knew of. Of course, he may have I suppose. When he was arrested, the old trailer was boarded up and no one but teenagers ever ventured on that land. I can't imagine he had the money for a horse, though. He didn't strike me as being able to afford much more than the basics.

"Follow me. We have most of our articles from that time period on discs." I followed her into a room with three computers at desks. She sat down, inserted a CD, and keyed in his name, 'Dolphin World', and 'arrest record' in the search bar.

Instantly, several sites popped up, all articles from the *Kumsquat Standard.*

"Have fun," she said.

I didn't have a whole lot of time, but am fortunately a fast reader. The first article title was 'Dolphin World Trainer Implicated in Dolphin Release to Suwannee'.

Matthew Parks has been detained and questioned by Kumsquat Police in the unauthorized release of a trained dolphin from Dolphin World Encounter Park. The dolphin, known and loved as a favorite in the dolphin encounter park, was reported missing early Monday, June 3rd. Matthew Parks was scheduled to work that day, and had been reported as passing several riverside homes near the park in his motor boat shortly before sunrise. Mr. Parks regularly traveled that route in his work as a trainer at the park, but residents reported that he usually passed by several hours later.

He did not report to work that morning, when park owner, Billy Astird arrived at 8 a.m. The park pools are fed by the Suwannee River, though the gates that open to the river were securely closed and locked. There was no sign of tampering with the locks. Mr. Astird's keys were in his possession.

All of the other dolphins were accounted for, and unharmed.

"We have no idea how Flash could have gotten out, or how anyone could have had access to the gates that open to the river."

Police speculate that someone who had access to the keys had copied them, and then released the dolphin through the gate early this morning. Area locksmiths and key makers are being questioned. Mr. Parks is a person of interest in the case.

Matthew Parks sounded like a hero to me. The next two articles restated a lot of the information I'd already seen in the first article. The third article mentioned that a warrant out for Mr. Park's arrest had been issued, and the reporter said there was speculation that the key had been reproduced at a small hardware store in nearby Elkin. The store employee identified Mr. Parks in a police line-up as the key owner.

I glanced at the wall clock. I only had a few minutes left. However, when my eyes fell on the next two paragraphs, nothing was gonna drag me away!

Police inspected Mr. Parks' home, which has remained empty since the dolphin escape. Of interest were several magazines delineating the concerns of animal activists regarding dolphin petting enclosures and their dangers to the welfare of dolphins.

Police Chief, Robert Myers stated, "We have enough evidence at this point, and a warrant has been issued for the arrest of Matthew Parks. There have been scattered reports of a man that resembles Mr. Parks in the upper region of the Suwannee, exercising race horses by trailing them behind his motorboat.

Anyone with information, please call the Kumsquat Police Department at 770-935-7995.

I wanted so badly to read the next article, but it would have to wait. I would be lucky to make it back on time if I ran as fast as I could. I asked the librarian on my way out if she could save the links for me and that I would be back later.

Unfortunately, I knew I couldn't return that day, since my animals counted on me for sustenance. I would spend lunch hour the next day reading through the last few articles.

Why would he have been exercising racehorses in the water? I guess he had to make a living, but this was the craziest story I'd ever heard. Maybe dolphin training isn't all that different from horse training.

Of course none of this made sense to me, knowing nothing about dolphins. How did Flash find his way to Matthew Parks' area of the river? Matthew was initially detained by the police and presumably took off to the northern Suwannee to exercise race horses before his arrest. This of course begged the question: was my Lightning an old race horse???

I was thrilled to see Hank was still at my trailer, finishing up with the AC. It was almost as thrilling as dragging my sweaty body up the stoop and opening the door to a blast of cold air.

"Ahhhh!" I collapsed on the couch, soaking in the cool air.

Hank must have just finished. He was gathering his tools.

"You might get away with keeping the bedroom door open at night. Just keep it closed during the day so the unit doesn't overwork."

"Thank you." I let the cold air sift over me, but only for a moment before springing upright.

"I found out Matthew Parks worked with horses."

"Who is Matthew Parks?"

"The owner of this place. The dolphin trainer."

"Oh…I thought the name was familiar. Good job. How did you find that out?"

"I read some articles at the library. I'll read more tomorrow but he was sighted miles away up the Suwannee exercising race horses in the river! He dragged them behind his boat! There were sightings of him and the horse soon after Flash was released."

"Did they describe the horse?"

"Not in the article I read. I hope they will in the next one. But if it was really him…the horse didn't have much time to meet Flash. And how did Flash know to come here? The article said the race horse was being exercised in the northern Suwannee."

"You said he was in his boat when he released Flash. He must have returned here in his boat. Flash had been in Dolphin World for years. Maybe since Matthew Parks was the only person he knew well since Matthew was his trainer, he followed his boat."

Lightning whinnied, and I jumped up to look out the window.

"Flash!"

I shot out the door, with Hank behind me. Lightning had stepped up to her knees in the water, and was tossing her head up and down. The dolphin approached her, and imitated the head movements.

"Well. If Lightning was the race horse, maybe Matthew brought her here. If Flash followed Matthew here, maybe that's how he met Lightning." Far-fetched. First, why would any racehorse owner let Matthew bring the horse to his single wide trailer, and second, Lightning showed not one molecule of racehorse physique. Time can be cruel…but still.

"Or maybe he owned Lightning." Hank's brow furrowed like a newly plowed field as he tried to sort out any half plausible reason that the horse and dolphin had somehow met. "Maybe once Matthew was arrested, Lightning just stayed here…and this is where she's been all this time. It seems impossible…but then, so does the fact that she is friends with a dolphin at all!"

Zippy was screaming at us to let him out of his pen.

"I'll get him," Hank offered.

I was grateful. Flash was not here every day, and never lingered long. I loved the few moments I got to see him. And if the story I'd imagined was true, it was even more enchanting. I mean, a twenty-year friendship between a horse and a dolphin! How awesome is that?

Lightning had done some surprising things, for sure, but what she did next was the strangest. Flash turned and swam slowly into the depths of the river, and then chattered dolphinese to Lightning. Immediately, Lightning walked into the water till it was up to her shoulders and then she began swimming.

I know. Call me a liar or accuse me of smoking some hallucinogen. I am not kidding. What would I have to gain by making you think I am nuts? My jaw dropped to my knees.

Lightning's head and upper neck were all that stayed above the water, and you could tell it was a real workout. She was huffing and puffing. She didn't swim very far. Flash stayed right beside her. She decided before having a heart attack to turn back to shore, and was just pulling herself out of belly deep water when Hank returned.

"Now that's just crazy," he said.

The puppy was leaping at my ankles, overjoyed to see me. I scooped him up and while I held the squirming ball of fur in my arms, glanced back at the river. Flash was gone. The brief visit was all we were to get that evening.

Lightning came back on shore and shook droplets off her like a dog after a bath. Hank stared at her, shaking his head.

"There is something else you might want to check."

I tipped my head in his direction, but kept my eyes peeled on the water. Did Flash really show up only to entice Lightning to cool off?

"There are some pretty wealthy horse farms not too far from here. Race horses are stabled there. Because Florida is so hot, some of the owners do exercise the horses by having them swim behind motorboats in the river. I wonder if one of them has a record of Matthew Parks working for them."

"You don't think Lightning was a race horse, do you?"

We both looked at Lightning. A couple of decades can change anyone, but she was about as un-racehorse-like as any horse I'd ever seen.

"While you're at the library tomorrow, see if you can find any articles about exercising horses in the Suwannee."

I had a rough time making it through work the next day till lunch time. The librarian greeted me this time like an old friend. Her name badge said "Miss Templeton".

"Hello young lady!" she said, "I wrote the links to the three other articles for you right here." She handed me a post-it note.

"Thank you."

She led me to the computer room, and logged on, loaded the CD again, then moved away from the monitor.

"Have fun with your research."

I was already eyeball deep in reading.

Kumsquat police responded to a call yesterday by a homeowner in White Springs, Florida. A man was sighted July 5th, matching the description of suspected dolphin kidnapper, trainer Matthew Parks, implicated in the release of Flash, the popular dolphin from Dolphin World last month. The man was on the Suwannee, apparently exercising a horse behind his small motorboat.

The owner of White Springs Stable, Drew Larimore, well known for breeding thoroughbreds, was contacted by police. Further investigation revealed that Matthew Parks had been working for Larrimore's stable the past seven years in this unusual exercising technique. Parks developed the technique with his own horse to keep her in shape during the hot Florida summers.

"He was incredible with the horses. Some were nervous about the river, but he had a way with animals," Mr. Larrimore said.

Mr. Parks was detained by the police when he reported for work at Larrimore's stable on July 7th. He was arraigned in circuit court. Trial date pending.

I finished the other two articles and sat back, rubbing my eyes. I'd hoped there would be a description, or further information about Matthew Parks' horse, but there wasn't.

It didn't really matter. We couldn't prove it, but nothing else made sense. Lightning was Matthew's horse, and Flash was the same dolphin released twenty years ago. I felt certain of it, as unbelievable a story as it was. We'd never know if Lightning had remained by the trailer home all those years, or if maybe someone else had cared for her part of the time.

Could a horse really survive on a diet of marsh grass and that putrid water? I fed that question into the library computer. You will not believe it. Not only *can* they, but there is a living herd of such horses on Assateague Island off the coast of Virginia! Decades ago, a shipwrecked boat released the horses into the ocean. They swam to Assateague Island and adapted to eating the marsh reeds, and drinking the salty water. They all developed big bellies as a result, but thrived in their new estuary environment.

Then I plugged in a new search: Do horses remember human friends?

Get this. There was a study in 2010 that proved that horses make strong attachments, long term, and likely life-long with those whom they have had positive interaction with. It is a necessary behavior for herd animals, who depend so strongly on each other for survival. (If I sound like I am reading from cue cards, I was. Almost verbatim what the research summary said. Technically that is plagiarism, but I hope given my upbringing you will cut me some slack.)

I sat back. Matthew and Flash were Lightning's herd. She had no one else to turn to, so she stayed with Flash when Matthew went to jail. It had to be what had happened.

But what about Flash? Do dolphins form life-long attachments like horses? I quickly typed those exact words in the search bar.

They do. Dolphin groups called pods hang together for extended time periods. The article didn't say if it was life-long, but the same groups of dolphins had been studied that remained together for years.

Then I stumbled across the most interesting article of all. A horse trainer in Adelaide, Australia exercised horses by having them swim behind his boat in the Port River. He had lived on the water for years, and often saw dolphins. One day, he noticed a mama dolphin calving a baby, and she was having trouble pushing him to the surface. The man reached in the water and helped the baby dolphin. From that day forward, the baby dolphin was his friend, and swam with him right beside the horses he exercised in the water. He even had a dog that got along with the dolphin as well.

I could not have imagined a more unlikely story if I had made it up. I couldn't wait to get back and tell Hank.

Chapter Seventeen

Hank wasn't around after work, but my faithful friends Lightning and Zippy were. Flash even showed up for a few brief seconds. He made a quick circle nearby and then vanished. I guess he was just making sure we were okay.

We went through our usual routine, eating dinner while the sun danced its last polka in the treetops. Since I was up early every morning, as soon as the sun set, I was pooped and ready for bed.

That night, thinking about how unlikely stories are maybe *unlikely* but nonetheless *true*, I decided to peek ahead in the Bible.

I'd finished the first few chapters of the Old Testament - Genesis. It seemed like a good idea to now try the first book of the New Testament. It's a book called Matthew, and if possible, tells a story more unlikely than Noah and the Ark, *and* Lightning and Flash. It's a story about God sending His son…who is really just another part of Him, to be born by a human named Mary. That somehow made this dude, Jesus, fully man and fully God. A day ago, I would've slammed the book shut, but with the incredible story of my unlikely friends fresh in my head, I decided I was not one to scoff.

Hang on. It gets wilder. So Jesus was born with one purpose. To die. On first blush, a totally bizarre plan. But God, despite the happy promises after the flood, realized that His first impressions were right. Humankind was a total screw-up. They continued to defy God and think they didn't need Him, and ignore everything He told them to do. He had no choice but to kick them out of Heaven permanently, and let them fend for themselves since that is what they wanted anyway.

The thing is, God loves humans. I didn't quite understand *why* since most of what I saw humans doing not only to me, and to each other, but to *Jesus* was pretty despicable. God saw something worth saving though, so His plan was two-fold. He had to punish all the evil humans hoisted on each other, but He also wanted to find a way to have them return to Him of their own desire.

This is where it got a little murky for me, but I got the gist of it. Jesus was the scapegoat, the one who took on all the punishment we nasty humans deserved. In that way, He took care of God's need for just punishment of all the awful things we do. Like there is some cosmic scale and every wrong-doing must be punished, but it doesn't necessarily have to be the wrong-doer himself that is punished. God's need for justice could be paid by Jesus. It didn't seem fair to me, but I was willing to keep reading since it got *me* off the hook too.

All we have to do in return is be sorry for what we made poor Jesus go through on our behalf, and tell him we believed in Him, and understood this was the only way we could get back to God.

I had of course heard bits and snatches of all this growing up. But when I read Matthew, and the details of the crucifixion, and how gentle and silent Jesus was in the face of so much torture, I began to think of it in a new light. I knew what it was to be tortured, born into an existence where those who should love you instead tormented you. I am not equating my lousy childhood with what Jesus went through; don't get me wrong. However, his suffering made Him seem more personal, more approachable. He probably understood what I had suffered more than I ever imagined the all-powerful creator of the universe could.

It was really late by now, but the good news was I didn't need to get up early the next day. Saturday! I popped open my laptop and spent almost the entire night writing my story. Something about the book of Matthew inspired me to tell my *own* tale of friends of entirely different species managing to redeem and comfort each other.

It was 4 a.m. when I finally realized I was exhausted. I looked at my word count. 7,000 words in one night. My book was up to 25,000 words already. It was pouring out of me like blood from a wound.

It was a little hard to drag myself out of bed the next morning, but Zippy was definitely an early riser and was barking up a storm in the bathroom. When I heard him scratching at the door, I leaped out of bed. I couldn't let him destroy Hank's rental property.

Since I knew he would not leave Lightning, I tossed him outside and returned to brush my teeth and throw on some clothes. I glanced out every now and then as I got dressed.

Zippy was dashing in circles around Lightning, who was grazing on the 'lawn'. As Lightning nibbled at the tiny weeds, Zippy rolled over pawing and nipping at her muzzle. Lightning never got upset. She just lifted her head, till Zippy flipped over and boomeranged in another wide circle around her. This game continued the entire time I made our breakfasts.

I put Zippy's bowl at the bottom of the porch steps and he abandoned his torment of Lightning. Within a nanosecond, he was slurping his puppy chow. Lightning followed me to the hay bin, and then nickered, and chomped at wisps trailing from my arms as I returned to the front stoop with her hay.

I plopped her flake of hay on the ground and sat on the stoop. The story I'd spent most of the night writing was still swirling in my head. I don't know if most writers do this, but I could hardly wait to finish breakfast and get back on the computer. It was almost as though the story were a living creature in my body, clawing and pushing to be born.

I crammed a bowlful of Lucky Charms down my throat, then settled on the stoop again with my computer on my lap. It was probably hours before I stopped. I only stopped because I was getting hot and thirsty.

Hank showed up sometime in the midafternoon. My neck had developed a crick from all the hours typing. I was glad to see him.

"Hi Leah. Great day for a swimming lesson. You interested?"

I wiped the sweat from my forehead, and hit 'save'. 30,000 words. I'd written 5,000 words that morning. At this pace, I'd be done by August.

"Working on your book?" Hank asked.

"I worked all night, and all morning. It is like Noah's flood pouring out of me. 30,000 words! I'll be done a month early."

"You don't just write and send it in," Hank said.

"I don't?"

"Not if you want to win. First, you edit. You read it over a few dozen times and try to get rid of every misspelled word, or grammar error, or plot problem."

That didn't sound fun at all.

"But for now, you have earned a break. Today, I will teach you how to do the free-style stroke."

"What's that?"

"Like this." Hank demonstrated with arm and head movements. "You do that while kicking."

"We tried that already," I reminded him, "Remember I almost drowned?"

"In two feet of water." He grinned at me, and grabbed my hand. "C'mon. Nothing to lose."

"Except my life."

I put the computer on the top stoop and followed him out to the water.

You don't need the details of what transpired next. It involved a lot of sputtering, a few words I probably should not have said, and a good bit of drinking the Suwannee swamp. However, I did manage to swim by the end of our hour practicing. I swam at least ten feet without drowning or touching my toes to the river bed.

The swimming part was not the part that kept me lying awake that night. It was what happened when I finally free-styled my way to shore and sat down in the shallow river edge, pumping my fist in the air.

"I did it!"

Hank swam up next to me, flopped over on his side, and reached up to high five me. Somewhere in the middle of that innocent move, his palm ended up against my cheek, and next thing I knew, he pulled me down towards him and kissed me.

I am pretty sure he didn't mean to do it. It kind of just happened. I didn't really try to help it along, but I didn't exactly fight it either. As far as kisses go, it was pretty chaste. No tongue or groping or anything gross like that.

He pulled back almost immediately. I could tell he was embarrassed, and didn't know what to say. I am not often one to flop about sucking air like a fish when conversation lags, so I covered the moment with the first words that came barreling into my head.

"Great idea! I will throw some romance in the book! Thanks for the idea."

I shot to my feet, and hurried up the steps, snatching my computer.

"Be back after I dry off!" I called.

I'd forgotten I didn't have any dry clothes other than work clothes to change into. It was time to fork over some hard earned cash for one more set of shorts and shirt, and a bathing suit. I went into the bathroom, and toweled off my dripping hair. I took my time because frankly, *what just happened???*

The last thing I needed was to complicate my friendship with Hank by actually *liking* him. I mean, of course I *liked* him. But I sure didn't need or want to be *involved* with him. Not like that. I'd seen enough of what happened as soon as people started hooking up. Hank was the first real friend I'd ever had. Was it ruined now?

Fortunately, Hank apparently came to the same conclusion because when I finally emerged from the trailer, he acted like nothing had happened. Flash made that easier on all of us, choosing that moment to surface mid-river. Lightning and Zippy instantly shouted hello, and the three of them chattered away in their own language.

As usual, Flash didn't stay long. Hank left pretty soon after Flash did, darting only one quick uncomfortable look at me when he said he had to go.

With some time to go before I had to feed my little family, I settled back on the stoop with my computer and started typing.

He reached over, and the tips of his fingers touched my cheek. For a moment, I thought he was going to kiss me, but instead, he picked something off the back of my head and said, "Look, a spider is making a nest in your hair."

I can't write romance. And I surely can't *live* it. After scratching out that stupid paragraph, I continued with my more realistic story of when the horse wades into the water and starts swimming with the dolphin.

That's how it went for the next several weeks. Every spare chance I got, I sat down to work on the book in between work, swim practice, and feeding my crew. Hank showed up now and then, but not as much as he used to. It was okay. I was teaching myself to swim. He'd shown me enough that I could take over from here.

When he did show up, he didn't act too strange, but it wasn't quite the same as it had been before *the kiss.* I thought maybe I ought to just talk to him outright about it, but then every time chickened out when the opportunity arose.

Meanwhile, July slammed into Florida like a bug into a car's windshield. Pennsylvania was like the Arctic compared to a Florida summer. The air was so hot, it felt like my throat would burn if I took too deep a breath. I spent a lot of my free time lounging in the river, as did Lightning and Zippy. That took a toll on my writing time, but by the end of July, I'd finished all but the ending to the book.

Hank started coming around more, and sitting in the water with me. I guess he felt enough time had passed since *the kiss* that he figured I'd forgotten.

Which I hadn't.

"How's the book coming?" he said, as July melted into August.

"Done except for the ending. I just don't know how to end it."

Hank nodded. "Do you want it to be a happy ending?"

"I don't know. It's pretty much my life, and I don't know how it will end. I'm stuck right now with the heroine working a minimum wage job, and seeing no possible way life will ever change."

"Does she want it to change?"

"She doesn't know."

"If she could change it anyway she wanted, how would she change it?"

"She wouldn't still be working at the Better-Mart."

"Where would she be working?"

I settled back so the water lapped over my chest and nibbled at my chin. By the way, I had gotten a bathing suit and practically lived in it.

"Somewhere without people. Maybe with dolphins."

Hank nodded. "Maybe you really should think about getting your GED and going to college for marine biology."

"With what money?" I asked. "Don't colleges make you pay for the privilege of taking up floor space?"

I realized he'd tricked me into talking about myself instead of my heroine. But he did give me an idea. Maybe I would send my heroine to college. She was getting pretty boring with her job at the Better-Mart. Besides, I only had a month till the book contest entry deadline. And I still had to edit it, according to Hank.

However, Hank moved on to a new topic. "They are watching a tropical depression off the coast of Africa. It's early, but hurricanes do come sometimes in August."

"What do you do when one hits here?" I asked.

"We go North and inland. The Suwannee floods like any river, but during hurricanes, it has had some pretty big floods in the past. Not often, but the roads out of here end up completely under water."

This was not great news. Where could I go, and how could I get Lightning to safety?

"What do you think Lightning did during floods if she was on her own?"

"The wild animals know to get to higher ground. I guess that's what she did too. *If* she was on her own."

"What will I do with her if a hurricane comes?"

I had never had to worry about the safety and welfare of another creature before other than myself.

"We'll get her to one of the farms inland," Hank said.

"Do you know of any?"

"My Dad does. I'll ask around. She'll be okay. And lots of low pressure areas never become hurricanes, and most that do, don't end up hitting us here."

"When was the last time a hurricane hit here?"

"Hurricane Charlie in 2004 did a number on the Suwannee. It was Cat 4 when it hit. Some nasty flooding then. I was pretty young but I remember when we came back what a mess it made."

"Did it hurt the cottage?"

"The cottage was built the next year. Our house survived but lost part of the roof."

"What month did Charlie come?"

"August. Maybe you better finish your book early."

He grinned, and splashed some water on my face.

"Don't worry too much. Like I said, they almost never hit. If we have to make a run for it, you can tag along."

"Not without Lightning," I said.

"We'll figure something out."

All that talk actually gave me a great idea for how to end my book. As soon as he left, I raced inside. In one sitting, I had completed the rough draft. I don't know if I'd ever felt prouder of myself.

While I reread, and tried my hand at editing (which is *way* not fun, and I wasn't very good at it), Hank kept me updated on the progress of Tropical Storm Angelina. It was still a few weeks away, but some early predictions were passing it right over my trailer.

"What will Flash do in a hurricane?" I asked. It didn't seem likely that dolphins suffered in hurricanes, but I really had no idea if it affected them.

"Well since dolphins have to surface to breathe, they can drown since the waves are so rough in a hurricane. I read that they can sense the change in salinity of the water from all the hurricane rain, and they get out of the path if they can. Dolphin babies don't do well in hurricanes."

My face fell. I had not considered that.

"But there's another strange thing that happens with dolphins. Their normal cycle to be able to have a baby changes if their calf dies, so more dolphin calves are born after a hurricane."

Wow.

"I figure that's just another amazing example of God's fine tuning of the universe," Hank said.

"Or survival of the fittest," I suggested. I didn't really see the need to bring God into this.

Hank shrugged and didn't argue the point. "How's the editing coming along?"

"Terrible. I think I am just going to submit it. I've read it through so many times that I can't stand it. I am afraid you will be throwing your $200 away."

"Easy come, easy go. Go through it one more time. Then let me know and I'll help you submit it and fund your trip to fame and fortune."

Hank may have been joking, but it meant a lot to me that he had enough confidence that he was willing to risk money on me. Not many people had ever believed in me.

"Will Flash stay in the river then if a hurricane comes?"

"I doubt it," Hank said. "From all I've read, dolphins go to deeper water out of the path."

I looked out over the river. Often when we spoke about Flash, he would appear almost as though he sensed our thoughts of him. Not this time.

"Will he know how to come back?" I asked.

Hank turned and gazed at me, with sad eyes.

"I hope so. He's lived in this river a long time."

The sun was beginning to tiptoe in the tree tops. Dinner time approached. "Do you think he is lonely?" I asked.

"No. He has you, and Lightning."

Zippy barked, and make a running leap into the water. He had seen Flash's fin before we did.

"And Zippy," Hank said laughing.

Chapter Eighteen

I finished the book's final edit just as Tropical Storm Angelina got upgraded to a hurricane. Projections still showed the hurricane making landfall over Kumsquat, and there were murmurings of forced evacuations as the storm intensified. Great. Just *great. Kumsquat was about to become squat.*

The good news is it made me grope my way through the final edit a lot more quickly than I might have. Hank met me at the library, so we could use the internet, and we submitted my book two weeks before the deadline.

Not a moment too soon.

By the following week, all the projections showed Angelina following a track a lot like Charlie, the hurricane Hank had told me about that leveled Kumsquat a couple of decades ago. As the hurricane approached Cuba, Better-Mart told its employees they were boarding up the store and we needed to evacuate along with anyone who wanted to live. I'm not kidding. That's what they said.

Hank told me his folks had already agreed to take me and Zippy with them to stay with his relatives in Northern Florida.

"What about Lightning?" I asked.

"There's a farm about ten miles inland," Hank said. "The owner is a friend of Dad's. He said Lightning can stay there. He says they made it through Charlie, and he is sticking around for Angelina."

"How do we get her there?"

"He has a trailer. He can get her tomorrow."

Tomorrow!

"Can I stay there with her?" I asked.

"Leah, I know you have never been in a big hurricane, but it's crazy to stick them out. They usually spawn tornadoes, massive flooding…we need to go."

"What will happen to my trailer?"

I know what you are thinking. Who would care about a piece of junk like that old single-wide? *Me.* That's who. This was the only place I'd ever lived where I had felt a moment of happiness. Honestly, it was the only place I'd ever lived where I was pretty sure I *would* live till the morning…

"I guess we leave it in God's hands." Hank held out his own hands for emphasis. I sure hoped God's hands were a lot bigger than Hank's cause the hurricane was huge.

We hadn't seen Flash all week. Hank thought he sensed the approaching storm and had already left the river for the Gulf. I was beginning to hate Angelina. She was wiping out everything I cared about, and she hadn't even made her formal entry yet.

The next day, Farmer Hayworth (yes, that is his real name) showed up with his old horse trailer. I hugged Lightning and felt like my heart was going to break. I had no idea how she would act being led into a trailer, but she behaved as though she did it every day. Calm as could be. I wish I could say the same for me. As the trailer drove away, I crumpled in a heap of tears.

Hank's folks gave me a suitcase for "all my things." That kinda made me laugh. "All my things" filled about a third of it. I threw the Bible in on top of my tiny stash of belongings.

"Bring your computer, and we'll box up your Coleman stove too," Hank said.

That worried me. It was like he didn't expect to have them still be here when we came back. Still, I did what he said. He showed up with his folks the next day. Projections for Angelina hadn't changed one teensy bit. We had to leave.

Hank locked all the trailer windows and door, and shut off the water and electricity. I climbed mournfully into the back seat with Zippy on my lap. Mrs. Forrest peeked around the head-rest, and smiled at me.

"It will be ok. This trailer made it through Hurricane Charlie."

I hadn't thought of that! I smiled back at her, wondering if Hank knew he'd hit the parental jackpot.

It started raining on the drive to Hank's uncle. He told me that was the outer bands of the hurricane already hitting Florida.

"When will the hurricane itself hit?" I asked.

"Within the next three days if it is still moving on the path they expect," Mr. Forrest told me.

"Is your uncle's house safe?" I whispered to Hank.

"Uncle John is northwest of the projected path. We should be fine."

I didn't talk much for the rest of the drive. I was pretty worried about Lightning. Ten miles inland didn't sound a whole lot safer than the river bank, but Hank assured me it was. "The tide could rise with a storm surge as much as twenty feet."

I gulped. Twenty feet would put the trailer under water and probably half of the Kumsquat Oasis.

"Lightning will be fine where she is," Mr. Forrest said, "Bill Hayworth has lived on that property his whole life and never evacuated from a hurricane."

I was surprised that thus far, neither of the Forrest parents had asked me about my parents. Surely they assumed my parents were worried…like any normal parent would be with their kid in the path of a major hurricane. I can't imagine what Hank must have told them to keep them from pelting me with questions about how worried my parents must be.

I hadn't thought much about my parents since my escape. Now and then I got kind of depressed thinking of what life could have been, *should* have been. My birthday was coming up in a couple of weeks. I could not remember my folks ever buying me a gift. Once my mom gave me a cupcake. One of Mom's drug dealers found out it was my birthday and wanted her to give it to me. Big hearted junkie.

That was the only time I remember it as being a remotely special day. I only knew it was my birthday because when I took tests in school, they required us to put our date of birth. I had to ask my parents when it was, who had to look it up on my birth certificate. Nice, huh?

As though reading my mind, Hank nudged me. "Do you have plans for your birthday?" He said it quietly, so his folks couldn't hear over the radio.

I couldn't remember telling Hank my birthday, though maybe I did when we were having the discussion about emancipated minor. We never *did* do anything about that business. I guess we kind of forgot since everything worked out with the trailer.

"Oh sure," I answered, "I'm inviting all my friends over for champagne and Lobster Newburg."

(I am sure you recall I had no clue what Lobster Newburg was but it represented the unattainable…like a boatload of friends or champagne.)

"Maybe afterwards, could I bring you someplace I think you want to see?"

I squinted at him, suspicion rising.

"Where?"

"It won't be a surprise if I tell you."

"Well, okay. If the party doesn't last too long."

Hank smiled at me. The rest of the trip passed in silence.

Uncle John was as nice as the rest of the Forrest family. Almost as un-nosy too. He asked if I was in college.

"Not yet. I'm working right now."

"Great idea. Trying to stay out of debt is a smart move. Hank says you are interested in marine biology."

I liked that the questions allowed me to answer without lying. I didn't want to lie to the man who was saving me from Hurricane Angelina.

"Yes. Especially dolphins."

"Oh. You want to research dolphins? Anything in particular about them that interests you?"

"Their friendships." This was totally true.

Fortunately, that seemed to give him all the information he needed, and for the rest of our time up there, he didn't ask me anything else about my background. I appreciated being spared the necessity of coming up with a pack of lies. I suspect Hank had told the Forrests something close to the real deal. I can't imagine why else no one pressed me for details although I know it wasn't for lack of compassion. Compassion oozed out of them like slime from a slug.

We spent a lot of time in front of the television for the next three days watching the approaching storm. Angelina never veered. It's like there was a hurricane magnet in my kitchen 'cause that's exactly where she was heading. She hit four days later, and slammed right into Kumsquat.

The reporters on location wore bright raincoats and had to dodge flying palm fronds and horizontal sheets of rain. There was a shot of the Kumsquat Oasis office with the sign ripped off. It lay in a tangled heap way down the road, lodged against a fallen tree. The water was up to the doorway. No doubt my trailer was flooded if not washed away.

However, despite how terrible it looked on the news reports, the storm surge was only ten feet at the mouth of the Suwannee. Probably less upriver where I lived.

"That's not as bad as they expected," Hank's father said.

Fortunately, after ravaging my little town, Angelina took a sudden change of direction and went almost straight East before turning North, and petering out over the ocean. It was almost as though she had some personal animosity for Kumsquat, and after pummeling the snot out of that one city, decided to let the rest of humanity off the hook.

Another example of my luck.

Still, as far as hurricanes go, it could have been worse.

Power was out for only a couple of weeks. Since the storm hit during low tide, the surge was not terrible, and since the area was not very populated, there were only a handful of deaths.

Unfortunately, cell towers had been damaged, and we couldn't get through to Farmer Hayworth for a week. We were still waiting it out at Uncle John's, while workers cleared the downed trees and electric lines, and the water receded. I felt a little like Noah, waiting for the mountain tops to appear.

Finally, Mr. Forrest reached Farmer Hayworth by phone. I listened to his end of the conversation, holding my breath.

"Bill! Good to hear your voice! Glad you're safe! How did the farm weather the storm?" Long pause. "I see. Where was the break?" Another long pause. "How many escaped?"

By now I was leaning forward, and feeling sick. It was clear that not all was well.

"Yes. I'll tell her. We will help when we get back. Probably in the next few days."

When he clicked off his phone, I almost ran from the room. I knew I didn't want to hear what he had to say.

"It looks like a tornado hit the edge of his pasture. Ripped apart an old shed and took down a section of the fence. He'd let the horses in the pasture – safest place for them in a big storm like that. Several escaped through the breach in the fence. I'm sorry Leah, but Lightning was one that got out. They've been looking but they haven't found her yet."

I closed my eyes. Welcome to my life. I knew it had been going too well for too long.

"When can we go back?" Hank asked.

"Bill says a few of the streets are still partially blocked by trees, but electricity is back on in parts of the area. He's back on-line. He talked with some folks in Kumsquat. The trailer is still standing, and so is the fishing hut. The good news is the hurricane passed through so quickly that the flooding wasn't nearly as bad as they expected. We'll give it a day or two to let them finish the clean-up and head back. Leah, I'm sorry, but we'll do everything we can to find your horse."

I could hardly stand it the next few days, just waiting for the flood to recede. I don't know how Noah lasted *months* waiting. I reread Genesis 6-9 to see if I could gather some clues on how Noah managed. Honestly nothing popped out at me. Noah was 600 years old when he built the ark. Maybe he had obtained wisdom that a near 17-year-old doesn't have.

The only other clue was God promised him that after wiping out the rest of the earth, God would establish a covenant with Noah. I had to ask Hank just what that meant.

"It means a promise…like a contract between God and Noah."

"What was the promise?"

"That God would never again destroy the earth by flood. There were other things too. Noah was to go fill the earth with more people. Animals would now fear people. People would now be allowed to put to death those who murdered other humans. And the rainbow would be a sign of the promise never again to flood the whole world."

I pondered that list. Most of it was terrible. Can you imagine living happily with a whole ark of animals for a year, and now they all fear you and want to eat you? And suddenly, in this new world, capital punishment is needed. I thought the whole point of wiping out the world was to start fresh with a better variety of human. Apparently not! The rainbow was a nice touch, but I'm not sure that promise would have been enough for me to wait over a year for the flood to recede.

Nothing much in the Noah story helped me wait for my own flood waters to recede. God had made no promises to me, and I had a long way to go before I was 600 years wiser.

Somehow, the time passed and we headed back to Kumsquat. At my begging, the Forrests stopped first at Farmer Hayworth's place. It was a mess! He hadn't told us how many trees had been uprooted. He said there had probably been more than one tornado in the area. Could Lightning have been pinned under a fallen tree? I was sick with worry.

We walked around the edge of his property, calling her name but she didn't show up. Mr. Forrest drove us around on the neighboring streets and we all peeled our eyes for a sight of her, but again, no luck.

Next we headed to the Forrest's house. It was still standing, and just missing a couple of shutters. A palm tree was toppled, but hadn't hit anything important. I was dying to get to the trailer, but the Forrests said we needed to unload our stuff at their house first, since it was likely the trailer would need some work before I could move back in.

As soon as we'd unpacked, Hank offered to drive me to the trailer. Most of the roads were cleared. Some downed trees had been sawed up and pushed to the edge of the road, not yet cleared. There was sand all over the roads. We finally made it to my spit of land.

It was obvious how high the water had risen. Right to the top of the undercarriage the trailer sat on. Hank told me the undercarriage was higher than most, probably because it was right next to the river. That was some good planning by Matthew Parks! The once white lattice that skirted the trailer was muddy and greenish brown. The ground was spongier than usual, but not outright mud. I dipped my head and said a quick prayer. *Please let the inside be dry.*

God had not bothered answering many of my other prayers, and honestly, why should He? I wasn't even sure He existed. Maybe He returned the favor. I prayed anyway.

My faith was rewarded. We opened the door to the same trailer I had left two weeks ago. Not one drop of water had ruined the new floor Hank had just installed. I almost cried. Except for the layer of mud on my 'lawn', everything looked just like it had. Well, the hay box was blown over, but Hank righted that immediately. Zippy's pen was also flattened, but it wasn't broken. That was easily standing again after Hank flexed his muscles with my help.

The only disappointment, which was *huge*, was no Lightning. I had hoped she would have found her way back here. *If she was alive.* That thought niggled its way to consciousness though I'd spent two weeks burying it. I had to fight not to burst into tears.

Hank told me he was going to dash over to check on the fishing hut. If I wanted to stay and poke around, he'd be back soon. He thought we ought to call the power company to get the go-ahead to turn the electricity back on, and promised he'd do that from the hut.

I nodded. I wandered along the bank towards the big oak tree where I'd found the rope so many months ago. It was the favorite walk for me and Lightning. Maybe she'd just gone for a stroll.

I walked for half an hour upriver. No indication that Lightning had ever been there. When I got back, Hank was sitting on my stoop.

"Power on!" he said.

I should have felt like rejoicing. Really, it could have been much worse. Instead, I just felt like crying.

"I'll run back to pick up your things and Zippy. If you want to wait here…I understand."

Again, no words managed to come to mind so I nodded. He patted me on my shoulder and hopped back in his truck. I sat on the stoop, looking out over the river. If ever there would be a perfect time for Flash to show up, it would be now. But he didn't. All alone on the trailer step, I laid my head on my arms and decided life sucks after all

Chapter Nineteen

Hank refused to let me wallow in my grief. Neither did Better-Mart. They reopened, and left a message on my phone to be sure I reported for duty the next morning. I really should be grateful, since the money was not terrible, but the first customer asking me if she could get a refund on her new patio chair ruined in the hurricane set me on a tailspin that barely landed safely to get me out the door at 4:30.

I sat on my stoop, watching the river and wishing Flash or Lightning would show up. Zippy nibbled my toes, which normally made me laugh, but not today.

Then I heard some honking, and the suck of truck tires on my drying plot of swamp.

"So birthday girl, ready for your surprise?" Hank rounded the corner with a wrapped gift in hand.

Oh yeah. My birthday. I had totally forgotten. At least I was one year closer to being an adult. Maybe things improved with age.

"This is for you." He handed me the gift. That made me want to cry. I had never received a gift before for my birthday. Maybe I did when I was a little baby, but I don't remember.

My eyes teared up, even though I really didn't want them to. Hank noticed, like he noticed everything, and said, "Don't cry yet. You might like it!"

I pushed my sadness back inside, and took the gift. It felt like a book. Slowly unwrapping it so the pretty red and white striped paper wouldn't be torn, I discovered I was right. It was a book.

A racehorse was on the cover, with a tiny jockey perched on his back. A palomino colored horse was by the race horse's side, and the rider of that horse held the reins of the prancing race horse. The title said, "Winners' Circle of White Springs Stable".

"White Springs Stable?" I paused, knowing I'd heard that name. Then it dawned on me. "That's the stable Matthew Parks worked at."

"Look carefully at the cover," Hank said.

I peered closely at the picture. The palomino horse looked familiar. Could it be? The rider of the palomino was a middle-aged man that also tugged at my memory.

"That's Matthew Parks!" I said. I remembered his picture from the news articles about his arrest.

"Is this…."

Flipping open the book, I raced through the first few photographs. The book was organized by decades. The first set of winning horses from White Springs Stable was dated from the 1990's. The time when we guessed Lightning was owned by Parks. There were several photos of race horses being led to the track by the palomino exercise pony.

"It is. It's Lightning, isn't it?" I said.

"She was in a lot better shape, but look at her legs. The same white stockings on three legs."

That was true. I rarely noticed Lightning's stockings, since she was usually crusted with swamp mud, but Hank was right.

"Did he own her or did the stable?" I asked.

"It doesn't say. They never mention anything about her. Only about the racehorses. But my guess is he owned her, and during the racing season, used her as the exercise pony. And look at page 15."

I thumbed ahead to page 15 and gasped. It was Matthew Parks in a motor boat with the palomino and a race horse tied to the back. The caption said, "Unusual training technique for horses with strained tendons."

"Why do you think Lightning is with them in the water?" I asked.

"I don't know for sure," Hank said, "But my guess is she was as calm then as she is now. She probably wasn't as flighty as the race horse, and it helped keep the other horse calm in the water. Now look at the next page."

I flipped the page. It was a different horse trailing the boat, Lightning by its side.

"Look at the water. Just a few feet back."

The picture was a little grainy, and not super clear behind the horses, but the dolphin fin just arcing over the wave was discernible.

"Could that be Flash?"

"I'd bet on it."

I shook my head in disbelief. We had solved the mystery of where they had met.

"But wait. Flash was only out for a month before they caught Matthew…"

"Look at the date of the photo."

It was a week before Matthew's arrest.

"Remember," Hank said, "There had been sightings of Matthew working racehorses behind his boat in the article you read."

"Then Flash didn't know Lightning very long. Strange they would keep a twenty-year friendship."

Hank nodded. The whole thing was strange but that connection was probably the strangest.

"I guess for a lonely confused dolphin, Lightning and Matthew became his pod."

I looked up from the book.

"Hank…thank you. This is the best present ever." I tried not to give way to the wave of grief that all I had now was a picture of Lightning, and that Lightning herself might be gone forever.

"Maybe Lightning found her way back to White Springs Stable," Hank said. "If you like, I'll buy you a birthday dinner to eat in the truck while we drive up there. Zippy can come along."

"How far is it?"

"A couple of hours. We'll be there while it's still light if we go now."

"Let's go!!!!"

I ran into the trailer to snatch Zippy's leash, and quickly locked the door behind me.

"Now we might not find her," Hank warned, "But it can't hurt to go look around and ask."

If I were writing the story, we would have driven to White Springs, and Lightning would have been standing at White Springs Stable gate, waiting for us. That is not what happened.

We found some stable workers and described Lightning, even showed them her picture in the book. They laughed at us. Told us that picture was twenty years old and it wasn't likely that horse was still around.

None of them had been there themselves twenty years ago, and none recognized Lightning. The owner from that time period had passed away a few years back, and his kids sold the place. The new owner would not have known Lightning.

We drove around the area as the sun set, just in case Lightning was meandering across some nearby field. No dice. On the way back, Hank bought me a huge milkshake and fried chicken sandwich. He even bought a small hamburger for Zippy who scarfed it down in about three seconds. It was the best birthday I ever had, and also maybe the worst.

As we drove, munching our food, Hank said, "I hope you are not too disappointed. I knew it was a long shot, but well…I thought we should try."

"I wish we'd found her," I said, "But I'm glad you found the book. And thank you for my first birthday dinner ever."

"Maybe we can track down the old owner's family. Maybe his kids would remember Lightning."

"Maybe."

I couldn't drum up much enthusiasm. Whether they remembered her or not, she had not made her way back to the stable. In all likelihood, if she were to make her way back anywhere, it would be to me. That's where she had been for several months now.

"I know dogs will travel thousands of miles to return to an owner," Hank said. "Lightning only has to go ten."

"Then why isn't she back yet?" I asked. "It's been three weeks. How would she know which way to go anyway? She was in a trailer."

"Homing pigeons can find their way home even if they are carried hundreds of miles away in a closed van."

"How do you know that?" I asked.

"I studied biology. Remember, it's what I want to do some day."

"How do you they do that?"

"No one really knows. But there are dogs and even some cats that have found their way home after several weeks over a long distance. Animals have some sixth sense about direction. Monarch Butterflies travel 3,000 miles to escape the cold in winter, and then fly back in the summer."

Now that was pretty amazing. A horse probably has more brains than a monarch butterfly. I appreciated Hank's sunny optimism. Really. However, if you want to know the truth, I didn't share it. Farmer Hayworth had been looking all over the place, and even posted flyers in his area. No one had seen Lightning. Again, she only had to go ten miles to make it home. The monarch butterfly could probably do that in an hour.

"I hope she isn't starving somewhere."

"She lived twenty years on swamp reeds," Hank reminded me, "I doubt food will be a problem."

We sat quietly, munching our million calorie meal. Zippy burped. That helped break the sadness a little.

"Do you think Flash will come back?" I asked.

"He came back after Hurricane Charlie," Hank said. That was a good point. I hadn't thought of that.

I slurped the last drops of my milkshake.

"I wish I could have made it a happier birthday," Hank said.

I turned to look at him. I felt like a heel. Here I was being all mopey-dopey after he had tried so hard to make my day special. It sure wasn't his fault Lightning was lost.

"This is the happiest birthday I ever had." That was true, too, though I didn't add the detail that it was probably the first birthday where I didn't trip over my folks in a pool of vomit and discarded needles. The bar sure wasn't very high.

It was dark by the time we rolled into my home-sweet-swamp. Zippy had fallen asleep on my lap. I cuddled him up in my arms as I opened the door and stepped out.

"Thanks for everything, Hank. I mean it. I have nothing to complain about. It's not like I owned Lightning. He was just a gift horse."

"You should never look those in the mouth."

I didn't know that particular saying, so just figured this was a special piece of wisdom I didn't quite understand. I'd give anything to look my gift horse in the mouth again, but I didn't say that. I didn't want Hank to feel any worse than he already did.

Hank waved, and called, "Happy Birthday!" as he drove back out to the road. I put Zippy down on the spongy, matted weeds so he could pee before we headed back in.

It was really dark, and quiet. Frogs were peeping and croaking along the shore. The water slapped the reeds, and they rustled back and forth in the moonlight. Loons called to each other across the river, a mournful sound.

I gathered my tired puppy back in my arms, and headed into the trailer.

Chapter Twenty

There were two more hurricanes churning in the Atlantic in late August and early September, but both veered back out to sea before they hit land. I was sure glad about that. Hank told me not to be too relieved, since hurricane season was just starting. I wonder if Flash knew that, because he had not returned. It had now been six weeks since Hurricane Angelina, and no sign of Flash or of Lightning. I hoped that at least wherever they were, they were together.

That didn't seem likely, but then, nothing about their friendship was likely.

Around mid-September, Hank told me someone had put an offer on the fishing hut. That gave me a moment of sadness, but even if Hank offered me the hut free then and there, I would not have taken it now. My trailer was the place Lightning would return, *if* she returned, and there was no way I was leaving it.

September also brought school buses. That reminded Hank of his mission to educate me.

"You should take your GED test." He could be a mighty big nag when he put his mind to it.

"I missed the last year and a half of high school. What makes you think I would pass?"

"They have books you can study."

"That sounds fun."

"Does working at Better-Mart till they cart you away in a pine box sound fun?"

Well, no.

"Maybe I'll look in the library for that study book," I said, just to shut him up.

"Well look what I found in the back of my truck?" He pulled out a study guide for the GED.

I curled my lip at him, but took the book.

"It's pretty heavy." I hefted it up and down in my hand.

"I hear the GED is easier than high school finals."

"Do I have to know calculus?"

"Nope. Mostly just algebra and geometry. It's all in that book. I bet you could pass the test today. There are practice tests in there. Take one. See how you do and you'll know what you have to study."

"So once I pass the GED… *if* I do this, and *if* I pass, what then?"

"Then you apply to college."

"With what money?"

"They give financial aid."

"Won't they find out I am a minor?"

"Oh." Hank hadn't thought of that. "Then you wait a year. You apply next spring for the following fall."

"Where do I apply?"

"There are lots of colleges that have Marine biology majors in Florida. The closest is the University of Tampa."

"How far is that?"

"Two and a half hours…"

"I'd have to move."

"Yes."

I looked out over the Suwannee. No Flash. No Lightning.

"Can I bring Zippy?"

"Probably not. I'll watch Zippy, and visit you a lot. Besides, who knows what a year will bring? It can't hurt to apply. There are cheaper state universities too. They are further, and on the Atlantic side, but under $5,000 tuition."

"I don't have $5,000."

"You nail your GED and get a scholarship."

Sure. Easy peasy. Since I had become a little disillusioned with God and Noah, I had put my Bible reading aside so had nothing better to read at night than the GED study guide.

It was not as terrible as you might imagine. I loved to read, and some of the facts in that GED were downright interesting. Hank was correct. I remembered a lot of the science and history, and a bunch of the test was looking at charts and figuring out what they showed me. Even the math was mostly review for me. There were some tough physics information that I needed to study for sure. English and writing was a breeze.

I discovered that all I had to do was pass or fail. I didn't have to ace any subject. And if I didn't pass certain sections, I could keep taking them till I did. I needed to score the same or better than 60% of graduating seniors would score.

That sounded doable.

Hank was worse than a mother. He dropped by every few days, and nagged me about how my studying was coming, if I had taken any practice tests yet, did I need any help?

I told him if he asked again, I was chucking the GED study guide in the river. Secretly, I did take some of the practice tests. I am a little ashamed to admit I failed the math, but only by a little. I passed all the other subjects, just squeaking by in social studies.

"There's a test at the community college in the middle of November," Hank told me. "You want to try?"

I shrugged. I sort of did, since it would get him off my back. Even more importantly, I thought I had a shot at passing. "Maybe."

When I wasn't working, or studying, I was looking out over the river for Flash, or walking along the shore looking for any sign of Lightning. Farmer Hayworth dropped by and told me no one had seen Lightning in his area, and he figured my old horse might have decided the wild life was more fun than captivity.

I know what he really believed was that Lightning was dead. That was what I believed deep down inside, but I didn't dare discuss that out loud.

"How's your Bible reading?" Hank asked one Saturday as we were sitting on my stoop, watching Zippy barking at the shrimp jumping in the Suwannee.

"I haven't been doing much." (As in *ANY*.) "I've been too busy working through the GED crap."

"How's that coming?"

I glared at him. He knew I didn't want to discuss the GED.

"The deadline to sign up for the next test is today," he said. "And you can do it online."

What was there to lose?

"It costs $35 for each subject…$120 for the whole test. You can take the whole test at once…or just as many subjects as you want."

"I have to *pay* for this?"

"It costs less than a trip to Disneyworld."

"And it's so much more fun!" I scowled, then heaved a deep sigh. "OK. I'll give it a try. Just to get you off my back."

"If you pass, *I'll* give you the $120."

"Do I have to pass all of it?"

Hank considered that. "I'll pay for every subject you pass."

"Deal."

"Come on…I'll drive you to the library and you can sign up online there."

I admit I was pretty nervous filling out the form. In two weeks, it would be obvious that I either deserved to be called a dunce, or maybe I was smarter than I appeared. I don't mean to brag, but I always thought I had the potential to be brilliant. I sure didn't have the background, but somehow, that didn't make me believe all the terrible things most of my old teachers and my parents said about me. This GED test might smash all my positive self-image to smithereens.

Unfortunately, we had both neglected to notice there was a minimum age requirement. I had to be eighteen to take the test. We found that out after wasting a half hour at the library working on the registration form.

I slumped in my chair, and punched in *Exit* on the computer.

"Sorry," Hank said, "I should have checked that."

He looked as miserable as I felt. Who would have imagined I would be disappointed over the loss of an opportunity to take a seven-hour test and pay over a hundred dollars for the privilege?

"Oh well. I'll take you out for ice cream instead," Hank offered. "It's a whole lot less than the GED costs."

"I'll keep studying," I told him, hoping it would cheer him up. He looked sadder than me. "I probably would not have passed the math anyway. History was iffy too."

Hank smiled at me, opening my car door.

Lady Luck sure was not spending any time on my doorstep lately. Or really ever, except maybe for those few brief months when I had all my unlikely friends with me.

The ice cream was delicious, but strangely, it didn't mask the taste of all the disappointment. All I could see before me was another full year of squeaking by, working at the Better-Mart, telling customers how they could return the toaster they had dropped in the sink full of water and it "must have been defective 'cause it stopped working."

Hank dropped me back home with my chocolate marshmallow mustache. I trudged into my trailer for Zippy's leash. I listlessly walked along the shoreline to make my regular fruitless search for Lightning while Zippy darted in and out of the water. I reached the big oak where the rope had once dangled, turned around, and dragged my way homeward again.

I guess I was depressed.

Zippy hopped up on the foot of my bed, and curled up in a little ball. I lay down with a groan, and glanced out the window. It was not quite dark yet, but I was so tired that I thought I would just go right to bed. I didn't have to study at least. I had a whole year to memorize the pesky math formulas that kept dashing out of my brain.

Instead, I reached for the Bible.

Yeah. Roll your eyes. So cliché. I know what you are thinking. She is in the midst of an existential crisis, and the great God of the universe comes to her aid with a bolt of comfort and miracles that change everything.

Wrong again.

For to this you have been called, because Christ also suffered for you, leaving you an example, so that you might follow in his steps. I Peter 2:21.

Do you get what this is saying? I knew a thing or two about Jesus. You would have to live under a rock not to know that he died a pretty gruesome death. Well, this happy little verse says that his suffering is an example to us, so we can follow and suffer just like he did.

This was worse than Noah and the flood, and all the impossible questions that story raised in me. Tell me why anyone would want to follow this God who promised so much suffering as though it were a *good* thing? Hank had told me it was not good to just pull a verse out of context. He said you have to read the whole passage, and even compare it with other passages to really get the meat of what it meant. So instead of flinging the Bible down the toilet, which was my first inclination, I read to the end of the chapter.

He committed no sin, neither was deceit found in his mouth. When he was reviled, he did not revile in return; when he suffered, he did not threaten, but continued entrusting himself to him who judges justly. He himself bore our sins in his body on the tree, that we might die to sin and live to righteousness. By his wounds you have been healed. For you were straying like sheep, but have now returned to the Shepherd and Overseer of your souls.

I chewed on those verses for a while. His suffering was unjust. I could identify with that. For example, I was hardly Miss Perfect, but I didn't deserve the parents I got handed. The verse that yanked me to a jolting halt was he "continued entrusting himself to him who judges justly." Despite the miserable death Jesus died through no fault of his own, he didn't seek revenge, and he didn't punch out anyone's headlights…though surely as the Son of God, he could have. Instead, he trusted the one who judges justly. In spite of every evidence to the contrary, he trusted God, and justice.

I closed the Bible gently. Zippy heard the soft flop of the pages and creaked open one eye briefly.

How? How did Jesus do that? How could he look around at the evil that was tormenting him, all the way to his death, and still trust his father, who surely could have ended it all instantly? And how could he believe in justice when he was smack dab in the middle of so much injustice?

I didn't know. I sure couldn't. But maybe *that* was what I was supposed to be following. Not his *suffering* per se…but his *response* to suffering. He trusted God, and he believed in ultimate justice.

I turned on my side, so I could face the window. The days were still hot. Florida doesn't stop baking until October or November according to Hank. However, the nights, with the river breezes, were not unbearable. I opened the window so I could listen to the waves sloshing in the reeds. The moon was just starting its journey off the horizon.

I hoped I would hear the sound of a blow-hole spurting a blast of watery air, but I didn't. Still, the river sounds were comforting, and I think my snores were soon louder than Zippy's.

Chapter Twenty One

It had been a while since I had checked my P.O. box. After another tormenting long day at the Better-Mart, I biked to the post office. For the first time EVER, there was a letter addressed to me that wasn't junk mail or a bill.

The return address said*: Montezuma Books Writing Contest.*

Now, I suspect you won't believe me, but I had completely forgotten about the contest I had entered. Remember, in the interim had been a hurricane, a lost dolphin, a vanished and presumed dead horse, studying for the GED, and then finding out I couldn't take the GED after all. I had a few other things on my mind.

Maybe some of you would have ripped open that thin envelope as fast as you would step on a spider. You don't understand how someone who has lived with constant disappointment views the world. There was mostly bad news in my life. Very few surprises turned out to be Flashes, Zippies, or Lightnings.

I tucked the letter into my backpack. If I didn't open it, there was no opportunity to be disappointed. What I didn't know wouldn't crush me, or result in suicide.

I biked home, trying not to imagine what was inside that envelope. I hadn't realized I'd had any real expectation that maybe I could win that contest until I started thinking about what I would do with all the money. Then I would laugh at my idiotic fantasy, and remind myself who we were talking about here. *Me.*

I pedaled, squeaking the whole way. I still hadn't oiled my bike…ever…and rust doesn't just disappear on its own.

Maybe I'll buy a new bike with my money.

Oh, shut up. You don't have any money.

Maybe, I'll buy the fishing cottage with my money.

You are an imbecile. You don't have a vampire's chance in the sun of winning that contest.

Maybe I'll buy a horse.

That thought made me choke back a sob because I realized I'd given up hope of Lightning ever coming home. I usually looked forward to arriving home, releasing Zippy from his pen, and sitting on the stoop eating dinner together. Not tonight.

I let Zippy out of his enclosure, and he did his typical 500 yard sprint a few times around the lot. Then he added a few new scratches as he tried scrambling up my legs while I leaned the bike against the trailer.

I scooped him up and he washed all the dirt and disappointment of the day off my face. Fortified, I sat on the stoop and removed my backpack.

I was all set to remove the letter, but then thought maybe first I should read a few verses from the Bible. I don't know what sparked that thought. I had not read the Bible much (as in once) since the hurricane and the loss of my friends.

I had kind of lost interest in God since He appeared to have lost interest in me. However, in a moment of superstition, I thought I should prepare myself with whatever was in the envelope with some bolstering. Hank insisted the Bible was God's way of bolstering us for the battle of life. I would call His bluff.

I ran in for the Bible, throwing my backpack inside the door, and settled back on the stoop. I am sorry to report I had only gotten as far as Genesis 11. I was disappointed to see Noah die at the end of Genesis 9, even at the ripe old age of 950. There was no big eulogy either. The Bible just says, "Noah lived a total of 950 years, and then he died." Pretty anti-climatic, if you ask me. You would think after all Noah had gone through for God, there would have been some sort of ceremony with a moving speech about how wonderful faithful old Noah had been. Nope. Just this: *And then he died.*

Genesis 10 just about put me to sleep, listing the names of Noah's sons and grandsons, and how long each of them lived. God could use a lesson or two on exciting plot development. It wasn't just the hurricane that stalled my Bible reading.

Genesis 11 showed promise. The descendants of Noah didn't seem to inherit his righteousness and they set out right away making trouble. They built a tower into heaven, with the somewhat ludicrous goal of tackling God out of His position as Supreme Commander. God had expressly told Noah that his descendants were to go populate the earth, but kids will be kids! Instead, they got this bright idea to storm heaven, and ignore His order to scatter and fill the earth.

God was having none of this nonsense, and confused them by making them all speak a different language. They couldn't understand each other, so gave up the whole silly tower idea, and went off looking for someone else who could understand what they were saying.

At least that's my take on what happened. I could be wrong.

Genesis 12 peaked my interest even more. A dude named Abram is now introduced, and I got the sense right away that he was at least as important to God as Noah had been. Listen to this:

The Lord had said to Abram, "Go from your country, your people and your father's household to the land I will show you.

I will make you into a great nation,
and I will bless you;
I will make your name great,
and you will be a blessing.
I will bless those who bless you,
and whoever curses you I will curse;
and all peoples on earth
will be blessed through you."

The overuse of the word 'bless' aside, this was pretty intriguing stuff. What was so special about Abram that God set him apart for all this special treatment? We aren't given a clue in Genesis 12.

Something struck me especially strongly reading these verses. God chose Abram and ordered him to leave his land, his folks, and all he knew to go to a place God would reveal later! Now not to sound immodest, or like I am comparing myself to someone who is mentioned with a gazillion *Blesses* attached to him, but *I* had also left my folks, my land, and all that was familiar to go to an unknown destination. Not that God had specifically *called* me like He did Abram. Still. I got the eerie feeling that God was telling me it would be all right. That somehow I had landed just where He wanted me to be.

I wanted to keep reading, since I was feeling hopeful all of a sudden. However, Zippy started raising a huge ruckus, barking like the sky was raining dog biscuits. I ripped my eyes away from my new hero, when I heard the telltale whoosh of watery air.

Out in the middle of the Suwannee was the unmistakable flipper of a dolphin…but it was NOT Flash. This one had a small notch in the fin, but much higher up than the notch in Flash's fin. And beside it, suddenly a very small fin surfaced, just briefly.

A baby dolphin!

I could hardly contain myself. I had never seen a baby dolphin before! There was a pinkish cast to the grey skin. They both remained far out, in the middle of the river, surfacing every few seconds. I crept to the shore and picked up Zippy, shushing him. Fortunately, he did quiet down.

I didn't dare breathe. The only dolphin I had ever seen in my river had been Flash. Maybe these two had gotten lost in the hurricane. Then I remembered Hank had told me that after hurricanes, the baby dolphin population increases. God's way of replacing the babies that die in the churning waves.

I stood on shore, petting Zippy, with tears flowing down my face. Then, as if blessings weren't pouring forth in enough abundance, another fin surfaced. This one I recognized instantly! Flash!

Flash was a father. At least, that was my guess. He had brought his new family to meet me. I was as certain of that as I was that the moon was not made of cheese. (Though I guess I am not actually certain of that…) He lifted his nose out of the water, and called out, "Eheheheh!"

That made my tears flow even harder because there was no answering horse this time. But I wasn't ungrateful. Really. Flash was back and with a bonus I never expected.

The three of them must have found a good shoal of fish because they circled and surfaced constantly, in the midst of a lot of bubbles and swirling water. I sat down, with Zippy in my lap, feeling like the world was *almost* exactly as it should be. There was just one horse-sized gap in perfection.

Then Flash swam closer to shore, and leaped into the air. He crashed down, and resurfaced almost instantly. Again, he lifted his snout, looking at me, and called, "Eheheheh!"

I laughed. All right! I can play this game!

I stood up, cupped my hands and took a deep breath.

Before I could make a sound, I heard a whinny that sounded surprisingly similar to the dolphin's call.

Knowing before even swinging around, I turned and saw her. I put Zippy down and raced to my horse. She was skinnier, dirty, and covered with burrs but it was Lightning. She'd come home.

I crashed against her neck. She seemed as happy to see me as I was to see her. By now, I was all out bawling, rubbing my wet cheeks against her. Our tears and mud mingled. She nickered and nuzzled me, nibbling at my shoulder with little horse kisses.

By the time I had recovered enough to look up again, Flash and his family were gone. Zippy was nipping at Lightning's hooves and barking to get her attention. She lowered her head, and blew a blast of air in his face, sending him back on his haunches.

If joy were made of atoms, the whole universe would not have been big enough to hold it all.

"Where were you?" I asked.

She didn't answer. She didn't even give me a clue. Wherever it was, they had not fed her much, or used a brush. I didn't stop hugging her neck for at least a half an hour. It was way past all our dinner times when I finally dared to let loose.

I raced to the hay stand Hank had made and pulled out a triple portion of hay. Today was a day of celebration. Besides, I'd been at Better-Mart four months now, and gotten a fifteen cent raise. I could afford extra hay. My horse was home!

While she lit into her hay, I went in and filled Zippy's bowl with puppy chow. I made me a peanut butter sandwich. I didn't want to waste any time inside making dinner.

That was maybe the happiest evening of my life. I sat on the stoop, my best friends near me. We finished eating and watched the sun set over our river. Flash didn't come back, but I knew he would now, eventually. Even if he didn't, I thought I would be ok. I'd miss him, but knowing he had a family of his own at last was a huge comfort.

As the moon rose, Lightning came over and dropped her muzzle in my lap. While I leaned my head against hers, she closed her eyes.

She was worn out. I wish she could talk and tell me her adventures, but instead she breathed warm, hay scented breaths against my thighs. I sucked in the smell of her like it was ice cream. I could not get enough of it.

Honestly, I didn't want to go inside to go to bed. I sat on the stoop till the mosquitoes drank at least half of my blood supply.

"Don't go away again," I whispered to Lightning.

She nickered softly and rubbed her soft muzzle against my arm. I think she was agreeing that she would stay put. I gathered Zippy in my arms, and headed back inside.

Just inside the door, on the floor where I had tossed it back in the days when my world was still a mess was my backpack.

Oh yes. *The letter.*

I would not open it tonight. This evening would forever be the one perfect day in my life. No sense marring it. Not tonight.

Chapter Twenty Two

If you were me, you would have been up at the crack of dawn ripping that envelope open. Again, I am sorry to disappoint you. I was indeed up at dawn, but side-stepped like a crab around the backpack as though it were about to attack me.

See, in a sense, it was. I knew I could not win the contest. It was the first book I had ever written, and I was a nobody from nowhere, and a high school dropout to boot. People like that don't win contests. They rot in jail, or in pools of vomit, like my folks.

The moment I would open the envelope and see the words that I knew were there: *we regret to inform you*….I would be booted from the mountain top I'd been on yesterday. I just could not come down. Not yet.

So I dressed, and with the tips of my fingers, lifted my backpack like it was poison, and carried it to my bike basket.

Lightning greeted me as though nearly two full months had not passed since I'd last seen her. She ripped into her hay with gusto. I again gave her three full sections. I'd call Hank and see if he could pick up a couple of new bales for me this week.

It was not easy to pedal off to the Better-Mart. While I refused to tie Lightning even after how my heart had broken over her absence, I was filled with uncertainty. Would she be there when I returned from work?

As usual, nothing worth reporting happened in the endless hours as a Better-mart cashier. There was one exciting moment when a code-blue was called. That meant someone was in some sort of medical emergency and we were to distract customers and keep them from panicking and causing even more code-blues.

The lady who was checking out her five bags of potato chips, two six-packs of cola, and a large container of Gummi Worms asked me, "Does Code Blue mean someone is in trouble?"

"Everything is fine, ma'am. They use that code all the time."

"Did someone have a heart attack?" Her brows were creased, which was somewhat amazing given the roundness of her well-padded face.

"Not yet," I said, eyeing her groceries.

She scowled at me, like she maybe got my subtle drift, and stormed off with her Code-Blue-Waiting-to-Happen grocery bags.

Some medics showed up with a stretcher and raced through the store at that point. It turns out it was for a little boy who had climbed on one of the display racks, and they had all crashed down on top of him. He was ok, though I heard later he had broken one of his toes.

The rest of the day stretched on and on. I daydreamed about the letter in my backpack. What if, for once, it was good news? What if I *did* win? What was involved in a publishing contract anyway? Would they expect me to write another book? I might only have the one good story in me.

It really didn't matter how many good stories I had in me. I didn't win, and I knew it. Somehow, I just knew it. If I'd won, there would have been a fat envelope, filled with information about all the things I needed to know now that I was rich and famous.

One skinny envelope for one sheet of paper with one simple paragraph: *We regret to inform you that no one was fooled by your pretense of being able to write a novel. Least of all us, professional publishers. Thanks for the good laugh.*

Finally, the work day grinded to an end, and I snatched my backpack out of my locker. I raced out the door to my rusty bike. Before unlocking it, I pulled out my pay-as-you-go cheap phone, and called Hank.

He answered immediately. I didn't call him much, but when I did, he never failed to pick up as fast as a hummingbird flaps its wings. It's like he was waiting for my call, which of course, he wasn't.

"Leah! How are you?"

"Hank, Lightning came back!"

"You're kidding!! That's fantastic! Is she ok? When?"

"Last night. And she's skinny…which is why I'm calling. Can you drop by TSC and get a couple of hay bales?"

"How about I throw in some grain too?" he asked. "This is a celebration!"

"Thanks Hank. I'd appreciate that. There's something else."

"More good news I hope?"

"Flash is back too! And he brought a wife and baby."

Hank laughed. "A wife?"

"He could just be shacking up, but it was definitely a mama and baby dolphin. The baby was pink."

Hank cheered. He'd known Flash even longer than I had and the news of the dolphin's return and new family probably made him even happier than me.

"I will be there soon," he said, "What great news!"

"One other thing…" I said slowly.

Hank must've heard something in my voice, because he said softly, "What, Leah? Is something wrong?"

"I got a letter from Montezuma Books."

"Oh. You didn't win?"

"I guess I'm not sure. I didn't open it."

"You are at the post office now?"

"No…I got it yesterday."

"And you still haven't opened it!?"

"I can't Hank. I'm afraid."

I was as surprised as you that I admitted that to him. As you have probably figured out by now, I prided myself on keeping my weaknesses to myself. The prey never shows fear or the predator pounces. I'd seen it a million times.

"Want me to open it with you?" he asked. He was nice enough not to laugh, or put me down. In fact, I think he understood.

"I would like that."

"Be there soon."

I biked home. Lightning was there, right near her old favorite spot under the tree by Zippy's pen. He was snoozing, and she was munching the overgrown weeds around the lattice sides of the pen.

As soon as Zippy heard my squealing chain, he leaped upright and pawed at the side of the pen. Lightning looked up as well, her usual cheerful, calm eyes settling on my face.

I dropped my bike and ran to my friends. I hugged Lightning's neck before lifting Zippy out. My reward was his usual face-bath. While he ran a few circuits around the yard, I grabbed the last sections of hay for Lightning, and plopped them down by the trailer stoop. Then I carefully removed my backpack and set it on the ground beside me to wait for Hank.

The river gurgled along with no dolphin fins breaking the surface. I hoped Flash would show up for Hank.

It wasn't too long before Hank's truck rumbled onto my lot. He unloaded the hay bales and brought them right over to the storage box he'd built. Then he returned to his truck and pulled out a bag of grain and a new pail.

"This is your congratulations gift," he said, heaving the bag on his shoulder and walking up to me.

"Congratulations for what?"

"For being brave. Lots of people talk about doing something big like writing a book…but never do it. It took a lot of courage to write your story, and enter that contest."

"Even if I didn't win?"

"Even then." He dropped the grain bag with a thud. "This won't fit with the hay bales. We'll keep it in your trailer till I build a grain bin."

Lightning was nosing the grain bag with huge, snuffling interest. We both laughed. Hank ripped it open and poured three or four cups of grain into the new bucket. I don't think I have ever seen Lightning more enthusiastic about anything. Her nose disappeared, deep inside the bucket.

"I better put this in the trailer right away. I think she could stampede us going after it otherwise."

He did so, then came back out and settled on the step below me. "So, ready for me to read you your letter?"

I nodded but I felt like crying. I had never really done anything very worthwhile in my life. The book had been my greatest accomplishment so far. I really didn't want to know that other people thought it was terrible. Rarely have I felt proud of myself, but until that letter revealed my inadequacy, I did. I had been proud of my book.

"You sure?" Hank asked, peering at me closely.

"I'm sure. Get it over with." I closed my eyes as I handed him the envelope.

Slowly, and carefully, he slid his finger beneath the flap, loosening the seal. Even Lightning seemed to sense the solemnity of the moment, and lifted her face briefly from guzzling her grain.

The paper crinkled as Hank opened the letter.

"Dear Ms. Grace…"

Here he paused. "I haven't really ever thought much about it. Your last name is Grace."

I nodded.

"Do you know what Grace means?" he asked.

"I guess…like thanks?" I realized I wasn't quite sure what *grace* meant. I knew some people, including Hank, said grace at meal times…thanking God.

"Grace means God gives us what we don't deserve. It is a wonderful name."

"That's great. Read the letter." My eyes were still squeezed shut.

"OK. Sorry.

Dear Ms. Grace,

Thank you for your submission to the Montezuma Publishing Award Competition. We had over 2,000 submissions, and the quality exceeded our expectations. You should be very proud of your accomplishment.

We regret to inform you…

Even Hank's voice wobbled on those words. I don't know if he really thought I was going to win the contest, but it was clear he was sorry to have to speak that disappointing phrase out loud. He paused and I cracked open an eye to be sure he wasn't crying. I felt bad enough for myself. I didn't need him getting all blubbery on me.

He was not crying. In fact his eyes were wide open and scanning the rest of the letter.

"It's ok. You don't have to read any more," I said quietly.

"No wait! Leah…listen:

We regret to inform you that you did not qualify for review in the contest as you did not meet the age requirements. The contest was open to adults only, age eighteen and above.

My mouth dropped open. They waited two months to tell me that!? And what about the entry fee? It had gone on Hank's credit card.

"The entry fee would have been on this month's statement," Hank said, reading my mind. "I haven't even looked at that yet."

"How did we miss that?" I asked.

Hank shook his head, still reading. Slowly, the horror in his expression began to melt away. "Let me finish. Listen.

"However, one of our agents was intrigued by your story, and asked to read it. She felt that had you been a legal participant in the contest, you would have been a strong contender as a prize winner.

Given your young age, and that this is your debut novel, we at Montezuma Books were all very impressed. So much so, that we would like to discuss the possibility of working with you to publish your book. Please call us at your earliest convenience."

I almost made Lightning choke on her grain because I leaped to my feet and shouted so loudly, "No way!!" I snatched the letter from Hank's hands and scanned the short letter. It was true. Every word that Hank had read was really there.

He jumped up as well and grabbed my hands, and we spun around in a pirouette, round and round till I was dizzy.

"You did it!" he said.

"I did it!" I echoed.

Lightning watched us, chewing her grain thoughtfully, and then dipped her nose back in the pail.

"You are an author!" Hank said as we both stumbled to the ground. My head was spinning in more ways than one.

I lay back on the ground as the world galloped in circles around me. Slowly, the sky settled in one place, and I sighed deeply.

"Do you think it's a joke?" I asked.

Hank chuckled. "That would be cruel."

"Should I call them now?"

"They said at your earliest convenience."

"That would be now."

Or it would have been…except just at that moment, we heard a huge splash and lifted our heads off the ground to see a dolphin leaping into the air, and then crashing back to the river. Hank grabbed my hand, pulling me upright, and we raced to the water's edge. Flash did three more acrobatic somersaults in the air, and then disappeared. His fin surfaced again, next to a slightly smaller fin with a notch high in the arch, and a tiny pinkish fin.

Zippy and Lightning both trotted over, watching the little dolphin family. My heart was so overwhelmed with impossible joy that I didn't even notice at first that Hank was still holding my hand.

Grace, I thought, glad I finally knew the meaning of my name. The dolphins swam in circles, while Zippy barked, and Lightning nickered and tossed her head. It was almost as though they were all congratulating me, but of course, that was impossible.

I watched them, and said a silent prayer of thanks. After all, God might be listening and if He was, He appeared to be my fifth unlikely friend.

The End

AUTHOR'S NOTE

I began this story, knowing it was a crazy concoction of fiction, flowing out of my brain. It combined all my favorite things: God, horses, dogs, and dolphins. I knew it was unbelievable, but life had thrown me some major curves, along with a cancer diagnosis. I needed fantasy.

I had completed well over half my book when I chanced upon a YouTube video of a fisherman from Port Adelaide. He exercised horses by pulling them behind his fishing boat. As if that wasn't interesting enough in light of my story, he had a dog that accompanied him on his boat, and a dolphin who had befriended him. The horse, dog, and dolphin are all seen with him in the video. Strange friends indeed! My impossible story was not so far-fetched after all!

I did not always believe in God. The whole God-story seemed too impossible to me to be true. However, upon the birth of my first child, I changed my mind. I began to see the miracles of His presence everywhere I looked.

It may be the most unlikely thing in all existence, but now I know God, and He calls me friend.

John 15:15

I no longer call you servants, because a servant does not know his master's business. Instead, I have called you friends, for everything that I learned from my Father I have made known to you.

Other Books by Vicky Kaseorg

Listening with a Broken Ear- 2011
God Drives a Tow Truck- 2011
Tommy- a Story of Ability- 2012
Turning Points -The Life of a Milne Bay WWII Gunner- 2012
The Illustrated 23rd Psalm- 2012
The Good Parent- 2012
The Well-Trained Human- 2012
Saving a Dog- 2014
The Tower Builder – 2014
The Bark of the Covenant – 2014
Poppy- The Dirty Ditch Digging Dingo – 2015
The Paws That Bring Good News – 2015
Joe- The Horse Nobody Loved – 2015
Gidget- The Horse Formerly Known as Witch- 2015
Gidget- The Horse I Didn't Own- 2015
Gidget- The Horse That Waited For Me- 2015
Singing in the Darkness – 2016

To Connect with Vicky Kaseorg

I love to hear from readers! Your comments and feedback are a continual inspiration. Please sign up for email updates to my publications at my Facebook author or blog page.
Visit my Facebook page and "like" it for regular updates on new books/writings/sales. I love to hear from readers!

https://www.facebook.com/Vicky-Kaseorg-Author-344952178879131/

Twitter:
https://twitter.com/vickykaseorg

Follow me on my daily inspirational blog at
VICKYKASEORG.BLOGSPOT.COM

Stay abreast of new publications at my author page at:
http://www.amazon.com/Vicky-Kaseorg/e/B006XJ2DWU
If you enjoyed this book, please go to Amazon, or wherever you purchased this book, and write a review! Much appreciated!
Also, reviews are critical to all authors. Please visit the site where you purchased this book. I would be very grateful for your review.

Sign up for mailing list of new releases and specials at:
http://eepurl.com/bp-EEP

Printed in Great Britain
by Amazon